MURDER ISN'T EASY

RICHARD HULL

ipso books

ABOUT THE AUTHOR

Richard Hull was born Richard Henry Sampson in London on 6 September 1896 to Nina Hull and S.A. Sampson, and attended Rugby School, Warwickshire. When the First World War broke out, his uncle helped him secure a commission in the Queen Victoria's Rifles. At the end of the war, after three years in France, he returned to England and worked as an accountant.

His first book *The Murder of My Aunt*, written under the pseudonym Richard Hull, was published in 1934. The novel, set in Dysserth, Welshpool, is known for its humour, narrative charm and unexpected twists. Hull moved into full-time writing in 1934 and wrote a further fourteen novels over the span of his career.

During the Second World War, he became an auditor with the Admiralty in London, a position he retained for eighteen years until he retired in 1958. While he stopped writing detective fiction after 1953, Hull continued to take an interest in the affairs for the Detection Club, assisting Agatha Christie with her duties as President. He died in 1973.

MURDER ISN'T EASY

RICHARD HULL

This edition published in 2018 by Ipso Books

Ipso Books is a division of Peters Fraser + Dunlop Ltd

Originally published in Great Britain in 1936 by Faber and Faber

Drury House, 34-43 Russell Street, London WC2B 5HA

AUTHOR'S NOTE

It need hardly be said that all the characters in this book are ficti-tious. I have however been nervous lest the name "NeO-aD" should resemble that of some actual organization. So far as I can tell there is no company or firm of that or any similar name, but if there is, no reference to it is intended.

RICHARD HULL

PART I
DESIGN AND PLOT

CHAPTER ONE

There is a limit to the extent to which the folly of any man can be allowed to ruin a business, and beyond that limit Paul Spencer has certainly gone.

But first I suppose I must explain what our business is, because its very nature makes it peculiarly easy for one man, by pure incompetence and obstinacy, by an absolute refusal to listen to reason, to render entirely useless everything that is done by his colleagues, however well *they* may work.

Ours is not an old established business, nor is it commonly classed as one of the learned professions. Nevertheless, for the promotion of trade, nothing is more important. We are in fact Advertising Agents—a profession which many people are apt to look down upon. They fall into the common error of thinking that it is clever to sneer at an advertisement; they consider that the proper thing to do is to laugh at them, and they hint that they themselves could write very much better ones.

I only wish they would try before they make that sort of statement! They would soon find out that it is not just a trick of style, a parrot-like reproduction of stereotyped phrases, but literary work requiring the most careful thought. Why, in writing an advertisement every comma is important!—and can you say that of a novel?

Then think of the artistic side of it. Not only have your words to be illustrated—and it is the production department of the agency that produces the idea, though perhaps you may hire someone to do the actual mechanical process of drawing it; in fact we have a man called Thomas permanently employed to do lettering and what we call lay-outs—but you have to consider the kind of type you will use, and the size of the type, to weigh up the pros and cons of which word shall receive the maximum emphasis, of exactly what arrangements and spacing of the words will be most certain to attract the eye of the public, carry conviction, and produce action. Not an easy matter I assure you.

But before I go on to demonstrate why Paul Spencer must be got rid of, perhaps I had better say something of the history and organization of NeO-aD (NeO-aD NeVeR NoDs is our slogan). It was originally my idea. I had studied advertising for a long while and I saw just where all the other agencies were wrong. They failed to study the sales problem of the client; their methods were not sufficiently modern, not thoroughly scientific. I had thought, of course, of attaching myself to one of the existing organizations and by exercising my personality, gradually grafting competency on to it, but so far as I could see, in all of them there would be too much deadweight to shift. So I decided to start my own company.

That very word "company" was the cause of my first mistake. I thought that it was necessary for a company to have capital, and that was a thing I had not got. Moreover, I thought that there was a great deal to be done by the secretary of a company, and so I got hold of Barraclough. Of course now I know that capital is really quite unnecessary. You just create some shares and some goodwill to go on the other side of the balance sheet and on you go. You can always borrow money somehow—besides one should never let oneself be kept down by want of cash. As for Barraclough's duties as secretary of the company, so far as I can make out he fills in one return a year for Somerset House. And for that I have saddled myself with having to give away a third of the profits that I earn!

Of course, as he is a director of NeO-aD, we do make Barraclough do something. He keeps the accounts for instance and arranges the contracts with the newspapers, what we call "space-buying", and looks after the general running of the office. Still we could have hired a clerk at two pounds a week to do that.

Barraclough, then, was my first mistake. My second was Paul Spencer. However well I might be able to design an advertising campaign, there had to be a client for whom to design it. I wanted therefore someone to go and find business. Someone who would get himself known, or rather who could get my work known, who could make people listen to him, in short who was a good salesman of the idea that NeO-aD should be appointed the agents of reputable companies.

After that all he would have to do would be to get their consent to the plans we proposed and keep in touch with them and keep them happy—take the directors and sales-managers out to lunch occasionally and so on—work which would take time that I should not be able to spare from my productive duties, but which surely was easy for an energetic, blustering type of man with plenty of personality and, of course, a reasonable amount of tact.

I must admit that Spencer seemed exactly the kind of man for whom I was looking.

I had known him for some time. He was a good-looking man of a fair type, rather fat perhaps, but that gave him an appearance (entirely erroneous as a matter of fact) of being good-tempered. He seemed to have plenty of life, plenty of bustle. He was, I knew, a little—how shall I put it?—coarse. He would never take 'No' for an answer, I was aware, but on the whole that seemed to me to be an advantage rather than the reverse. When once he saw a chance of getting the handling of a campaign into the office, I thought that he would never rest until the order was booked. Strange how when thinking of Spencer one falls into the jargon of salesmanship!

Up to a point I was right. I must admit that he is energetic, that he quite frequently brings in work. But what I had not realized was his incredible tactlessness. He *cannot* keep a client. Sooner or later he always goes and quarrels with him—generally sooner. Nor is he in the least persuasive. I supply him with ideas which any client must immediately accept if they were put to him in the right way, and he comes back not only without having convinced the man, but actually leaving him disgruntled. I have even known Spencer bring back alternative suggestions! And that brings me to another trouble I have with him.

I thought when we started that our respective spheres were clearly defined. Spencer was to keep his eyes open and find work. I was to do the work, and Barraclough was to make himself useful where he could—I am almost tempted to say, if he could. But I never expected to find Spencer making suggestions as to how a campaign should be prepared, any more than I thought that it would be necessary for me to do the contact work of the agency. Yet from the very first that is exactly what he did. To begin with I listened patiently enough to the amazing nonsense he talked, but after a while this began to pall. Besides one can point out the error in something which is nearly but not quite right, but it is impossible to argue about something which is merely fantastic. I began to find it harder and harder to counter his amateur suggestions for a selling plan, for, remember, he was always very able when it came to an argument. He never really had a case at all, but he always knew how to put it. Nothing would ever convince him that he would do very much better to mind his own business.

"My dear Latimer," he said to me the very first time I suggested it to him, "but it *is* my business."

As I write I can still remember vividly the confident tone of his voice. He was, of course, trying to make me lose my temper, that was one of his tricks, and he was very well aware that I hated sentences beginning 'My dear Latimer'. Besides, he generally used to call me Nicholas in those days; he only used my surname when he wanted to annoy me. However, I was determined to keep calm, and so instead of the direct negative which was the only real answer to the statement, I asked him in what way he thought it was his business.

"Your share, you know," I went on, "was, I thought, confined to getting work to do—just that, no more, except taking a third of the profits."

I could see that last remark had stung him. He must have known even then that he was not worth to the company what he took out of it.

He flushed a bit, but a little thing like that would not stop Spencer arguing. He even followed up my point, pretending to misunderstand it.

"Precisely, and I want to see that third as large as possible. Consequently it is very much my business to see that when I go to the Flaik-Foam people" (the campaign in question) "I have got something to show them which they are likely to take."

"I entirely agree. But what I am trying to suggest—I am afraid I cannot have put it clearly enough—is that it is my business to produce work which they will take; yours merely to go and show it to them."

"And you think with that I have only to go in order to conquer?"

I shrugged my shoulders. There was no need to put it so crudely as that! But that was Paul all over; always trying to put one in the wrong! It was unnecessary to imply that I was conceited. Besides, it was not true.

Seeing that he had hurt my feelings, Spencer shifted his ground cleverly.

"Let me try to explain on your own lines. You always tell me—

and I quite see your point—that you cannot produce good work unless you are convinced of the merits of the product. You're always preaching 'conviction' to me. Fairly enough, I own. Well, I'm the same. I can no more go and sell that caption 'One Flaik-Foam Makes the Bath a Joy' to old Macnair than fly. It's too long and it's got too many capitals. You see, *I* am not convinced. Sorry," he added carelessly, in a voice that expressed no sorrow at all, "but there it is."

I think it is very greatly to my credit that I refrained from striking him there and then. And what was the result of all this obstruction? An absolute impasse! He, if you please, refused categorically to go down to the Flaik-Foam people with what he was pleased to describe as second-class work and I, naturally enough, refused to draw up another campaign to be the butt of his ignorant criticisms until he had at least attempted to sell that one.

Of course it would have been taken. I had recommended the use of various of the women's papers—*Woman and Beauty, Wife and Home* and *Woman's Journal* if I remember right. Besides which there was a rather daring suggestion of the *Royal* and one or two other magazines; and the copy was some of the most arresting I had ever written. Barraclough had added a few figures and some rather good notes about circulation. He did that sort of thing quite well at times.

But as Spencer refused to take it along to Macnair there seemed no chance of its ever being seen. After a fortnight I hit on the bright idea of sending it all by post and explaining that Mr. Spencer very much regretted that he had been unable to bring it down himself as he had been in bed with a cold.

When it was returned without comment I was very surprised until I learnt that Spencer had been down the day before my campaign reached them and explained that I had done some work, but that as I (if you please) was not satisfied with what had been produced, he must ask Macnair to wait another week. Of course Macnair had said that Flaik-Foam must be put on the market at once and he could wait no longer.

I often see the Flaik-Foam advertisements. They take quite a lot of space in the daily papers—*Sketch* and *Mirror* chiefly. Not a bad alternative to the women's papers, but the 'copy' strikes me as very poor. If only Spencer had been more sensible they might be using our copy instead.

CHAPTER TWO

A fter that, of course, relations were a little strained. Not that openly there was any breach. To all outward appearances things went on in much the same way as before. There was so much to be done and we were so often bound to work together that it was impossible to do anything except work with external unity.

But naturally I could not forget. Every time I saw one of the Flaik-Foam advertisements I was reminded of what Spencer had caused us to lose. Each time I read the indifferent work that was being put in the press for them, my fingers itched to improve it. Moreover, though I am very slow to take offence, when once I do, I never forget.

Still there was, as I say, plenty to occupy me during business hours. Not that I ever spend a very great number of hours at the office. Very often I find it possible to concentrate more easily in the seclusion of my own flat. Besides, mine was entirely productive brain work in which, if you try to increase the quantity, you only decrease the quality. The routine work was no part of my business, a truism which, curiously enough, I could never get Barraclough to see. He was always in a perpetual state of flutter about dates when various journals went to press, and whether our blocks and stereos would be ready in time. I never could convince him that any paper will always really wait a few days. Barraclough, you see, was always a nervous, fidgety little man. I have often noticed that these figure men are very narrow-minded, very easily bullied by a printed statement that copy must be received by such and such a date. In short, slaves to the clock and the calendar. I flatter myself that my artistic spirit has raised me far above such pedantry.

But while Barraclough was as irritating as an alarm clock (and rather like one in the way he was constantly going off into squeaks about having blocks for the *Chemist and Druggist* by ten a.m. on the twentieth of the month) and so hindering me from turning out my very best work, Spencer was always trying to make extra work for me. I think he had a vague idea that if he kept me busy, I might forget Flaik-Foam. Of course he was wrong, and particularly wrong in the way he tried to extort work from me.

It was some weeks later that he came into my room, carrying a long type-written memorandum. It was one of his tiresome tricks that instead of saying anything, he had it typed, with the result that I never could get Miss Wyndham to do any of my work. He said—and it was a remark worthy of Spencer's tact—that it was typed to make sure that I should not forget it this time, an allegation in the form of a sneer which was most uncalled for. I had just once forgotten one thing. At least, he said I forgot it. To this day I am not at all sure that I had ever been told.

That, however, is beside the point—my memory is really excellent. To return to this particular memorandum. It was headed 'The Greyfields Canning Company'.

"Greyfields?" I asked. "Where on earth is Greyfields?"

"Oh, that doesn't matter. It's in Essex as a matter of fact."

I laid the paper down. "But it does matter. One must know everything."

"Suppose, then, you read what is there first."

Ostentatiously I pulled out a scribbling block and wrote on it, murmuring the words aloud as I did so.

"Greyfields. Somewhere in Essex. Where." I drew a line across the sheet and added brightly. "I can put down all the extra points I shall want to know as they come to me and we can discuss them all afterwards. Meanwhile, I'm rather busy———"

"Oh, no, you're not. You were only daydreaming, you know, when I came in."

By bad luck I had no papers in front of me and Paul Spencer's entrance had so completely broken my chain of thought that I could not remember what was in my mind. I know it was some extremely original plan for linking ourselves up with moderate-sized businesses which looked like growing into large ones, but it had entirely gone from my brain, I fear, for ever.

Reluctantly I picked up the paper and started to read it. It appeared that some people were thinking of starting a canning company in some remote corner of Essex. The whole thing was entirely in the air, but Spencer was so convinced that it would come off, that he wanted all sorts of things done as a pure specu-lation. He wanted Barraclough, for instance, to go into the figures of the proposed venture and get an idea of what capital they would want, and how much profit they might reasonably expect to make on each tin, so that we could recommend an appropria-tion of possible profits to be spent on advertising, so much for strawberries, and so much for peas, and so much for new potatoes —which was to be a speciality.

So far that was all good exploratory work, and Barraclough might just as well do it as do nothing, but then Spencer went on to suggest that I should prepare a complete advertising campaign.

When I read that I could not help laughing in his face.

"Glad you find something funny. What is it? Some typing mistake?"

"No." I thought I had better put it straight-forwardly. "Just the idea that we should prepare a campaign out of the air. You know as well as I do that would hardly be *scientific* advertising."

"Oh, I don't mean a final campaign. Just a rough idea to convince them that we can do good work."

"But that's exactly what we should not convince them of."

"Well, Nicholas, you said that—not me. I thought that you would feel certain that you could produce something for them. After all, you know, canners are easy. Lovely pictures of good-looking strawberries and luscious plums and bunches of parsnips fresh with the morning dew." It was just like Spencer's sense of humour to put in parsnips so as to bring one to earth with a bump, but that was a game two could play at.

"And then, having spent a good deal of time drawing these pictures, you find that they are not going to can parsnips at all."

"Possibly not actually parsnips, but every canning company does peas."

"Precisely." Barraclough, who had just come in, chipped in. "They all do peas. The established canners have got all the market there is. I don't believe a newcomer would have an earthly chance."

"Unless he advertised well. That's just the point. You see, what I want you to do is to let them know what they will have to spend to get their stuff well-established. In other words, how much spare working capital they must have, for of course for the first year or two, they'll have to spend capital advertising. So you could work out figures for them, while Nicholas here shows them pretty pictures."

"If I were to tell them," was Barraclough's answer, "how much capital they would have to lose, they would never start the company."

"There wouldn't be any need to put it as high as that. I thought we'd put it down at about five thousand a year for the first three years. Couldn't you work out something with that object in view?"

Barraclough nodded. "I see. Decide on the answer and then work out the sum backwards. That would of course be much the most accurate way of getting at the best advice to give them."

I dislike Barraclough when he tries to be funny. Still, I could see his point.

But as the discussion was drifting away from the really serious objection to the proposal, I brought it back again.

"And meanwhile I am to draw what you very rightly call 'pretty pictures'? Just pretty pictures in a vacuum!"

"Well, what more do you want to know? You'll find in there all the ideas that the directors have got in mind as to what they propose to can first."

"Lots of things. I want to know if they can really get the stuff, fruit, vegetables, whatever it is—chickens for export, do I see?" I flicked over the pages. "I want to know their sales policy—to wholesalers, to agents, direct to the public, by mail——"

"Quite a lot of that you would find answered there, *if* you would be so good as to read it through. And, my dear Latimer, *have* you ever heard of a mail order business in tinned plums?"

"Well, I only wanted to know. Then", I picked up the thread of my argument again, "I want to know what is the special advantage these people claim to have over their rivals. In other words, what is their selling point? Because, excuse my being obvious, that is what I shall have to lay stress on in the advertising."

Spencer shuffled about uneasily.

"I do wish you would not go straight to details. Get the general idea first."

"But one can't get the general idea until one has got the details. The whole science of advertising is to work backwards from the particular to the general. One must know every detail before one can possibly lay down the policy. It's very difficult to get the advertiser to see that, but surely you ought to know it."

"I've heard you say it enough times, if that is what you mean."

"Well, it seems to be necessary. The repetition, I mean."

Perhaps I did rather snap the last words out, and certainly Paul was looking furious. At any rate Barraclough thought it necessary to intervene with what he called tact. Poor little Barraclough, he was always pathetically obvious, and never more so than when he tried to be tactful.

"Just exactly what are the details of what you want Latimer to do? I mean I am sure you don't want him to go to the trouble———"

"No trouble is too great. I will not have that suggested." (Well, I had to protect myself somehow. Both of them were quite capable of saying that I had refused out of mere laziness.)

"—of preparing copy and lay-outs and art-work of all sorts which may not be wanted. Besides, you know, art-work costs money."

"Always harping on the money side! We must not let ourselves be kept back for the sake of not risking a few pounds. We must occasionally throw a sprat to catch a whale."

I saw Barraclough shiver. He was in a constant state of alarm over the company's finances. Sprats, in his experience, were apt to come expensive.

"Yes," I went on, "but the whale isn't even formed!"

"Don't mix your metaphors, Nicholas." It was one of Spencer's most maddening tricks to change in a second from a violent temper to a vein of broad good-humour. "Look, it's like this, I am well in with these people. I'm sure this canning company has a good chance of becoming a big thing—especially from an advertising point of view; once it gets started, all the advertising agents will be after them. I want to be in, not when the flag falls, but before it falls."

"And if it never does fall?"

"Oh, it's sure to fall all right. There's plenty of money behind these people—yes, I'm glad to see you both brighten at that—and I want to make certain we get the chance. All I want is a few specimen designs in two or three different styles———"

"Thank you very much," I interjected.

"—for labels round the tins, for trade-marks, show cards, in fact all the preliminary work. The actual advertising need not be so detailed. As Nicholas says, we shall have to get down to selling points."

"A few designs in two or three styles and an unspecified amount of copy. Have you any idea of how much you are asking?"

"A good deal, no doubt. But after all, you aren't busy. You might just as well do that as sit here doing nothing. As for expense, Barraclough, Thomas can do the rough lay-outs and give an idea of the finished art-work. We need not go outside for art-work yet."

Rather to my annoyance I saw that Barraclough was beginning to give way, but I really was not going to waste my time on a wild goose chase.

"I suppose," I asked casually, "that if we do all this the company will definitely consent in writing to appoint us as its advertising agents? And I suppose they will pay for the work we do?"

Barraclough instantly became technical.

"The company isn't formed yet. It cannot enter into a contract before it is. Though by a legal fiction———"

Spencer brushed him aside.

"And as for paying, I should think they would if they ever used the stuff. But they won't buy a pig in a poke."

That settled it.

"Nor will I. I absolutely refuse to waste Thomas's time or mine until things are more definite. Besides, you know quite well that preparing campaigns without being asked to do so is one of the things that the Institute definitely set their faces against."

"Oh, the Institute of Incorporated Practitioners in Advertising! Nicholas, Nicholas, you know perfectly well that when it suits you, you pour the utmost contempt upon them and maintain that you are far in advance of them, and are only going to listen to such of their ideas as seem to you right. But now, because it suits you, you quote them."

"Well, they may very well be right sometimes. And to my mind it happens that this is one of the occasions when they are."

"For heaven's sake, man, listen to reason!" Spencer was boiling with rage by now. "Here's a chance and you propose nominally on grounds of pure pedantry, but actually I believe out of pure laziness to risk the whole thing. It's as bad as the way in which you lost us the Flaik-Foam business."

"That *I* lost! Of all the preposterous statements! When *you* refused to do the tiny bit of work you had to do, you mean, out of motives of mere bad-temper. Every time I see that campaign that you threw away, it makes me nearly cry."

"There was no talk that time about not preparing a campaign until we were appointed agents in advance, or until Macnair promised to pay us for your stuff, however dud it was! And there wouldn't be that sort of chat now if it hadn't been that I brought the idea up. You've got two reasons and two only for opposing this. One is that I suggested it, therefore you are against it. The other is pure, bone idleness; nothing more dignified or intellectual than pure, bone idleness!"

"Well, so far as this morning is concerned, you have certainly wasted it. It is obviously quite impossible to go on discussing anything rationally in that frame of mind."

With that I got up quietly and with dignity, and put on my hat.

"I shall go out to lunch now. Perhaps you will not be quite so impossible later on."

Spencer looked at his watch rather pointedly. It was only half-past twelve, and I had happened to be a little later at the office than usual that morning, but I could afford to ignore the point. In the first place it was his fault that I was not still at work; and in the second, as I have said before, I refuse to be the slave of the clock.

CHAPTER THREE

I think that by now I have said enough for anyone to see what an impossible person Paul Spencer was to work with. Gauche, tactless, overbearing—those adjectives naturally sprang to the mind whenever you thought of him. But there were two characteristics of his which especially annoyed me—which must, I think, have been peculiarly irritating to anyone.

The first was his incurable habit of losing his temper one second and recovering it the next, and for two minutes being perfectly charming. At the end of that, as likely as not, he was insulting you again; and while this performance was going on, he expected everyone else to keep their temper the whole time, or at any rate to recover it when he did. He used to play that trick more often on me than on anyone else. I don't know what he took me for. A chameleon, perhaps.

But the second characteristic was even more irritating. He had an intolerable habit of twisting things round so as to appear to be always in the right. The remark about the attitude of the Institute towards preparing a campaign was a typical example. I was perfectly accurate when I said that the Institute, with a desire to raise the standing of the profession, had very definitely set its face against doing detailed work on the chance of getting it accepted. They took the line that you ought only to work when you were sure of being paid for it. And on the whole a very reasonable line. I mean, do solicitors walk up to their clients and remark that as they thought they might be wanting to make a will, they had prepared one that they thought was the kind of thing which might be adapted to their needs? Or do chartered accountants offer you specimen balance sheets? Or wave income-tax forms in your face? As a matter of fact I'm not quite so sure about the latter, but my point is obvious.

But there is a time to obey the desires of the Institute and a time to use common sense. The Greyfields Canning Company was obviously the first. The Flaik-Foam equally clearly had fallen into the second category. Yet, look how cleverly Spencer had managed to trip me up over the two! Of course a mere debating point, but still very irritating.

By now I think that it must be obvious, as I have just said, that Paul Spencer was extremely difficult to work with. But I was still a long way from the conclusion that I ultimately came to. As yet Paul had not made himself quite impossible.

That afternoon I decided that I was far too upset to do any useful work. One cannot work when one is disturbed. And so I took a stroll in the Park and thought over the possible means of getting rid of him.

There was first of all the simple method of calling a meeting of the company and passing a resolution that he should cease to be a director. For that purpose I should have to get Barraclough's support. I wondered how far I could rely on his intelligence? Well, that remained to be proved. It would be necessary to approach him when he was in a good mood. It would only require a little tact—surely it could be done?

But if by any chance Barraclough proved obstinate or stupid, or got some wild idea in his head about loyalty—the little man was capable of that sort of old-fashioned notion—then I should have to try something else. At that time I hardly knew what, though I was sure that something could be done. I think that all I had in mind was a vague, rather sordid, idea of buying Spencer's share. Though quite how, in the state my finances were in, I did not know. Probably I should have no difficulty in getting one of the banks to back me. I had read that they had money that they had difficulty in finding a use for. Meanwhile cooperation with Barraclough seemed the simpler solution.

Unfortunately the next morning found him in one of his alarum-clock moods. We had an old client, Henriques, one of the standbys of the company as a matter of fact, for whom we had been running the same advertisement in the provincial press for some while. It was quite a good advertisement, and personally I saw no objection to letting it go on, but for some reason they had suddenly asked us to vary it, for no better cause that I could find out than that they thought a change would be nice. A foolish idea.

However, stupidly, I had consented to do so. I had intended to do it on the afternoon of the day when Spencer interrupted me with his preposterous Greyfields Canning business, but all the excitement about that had driven it completely out of my head— which only shows how wrong he was to have said that I had nothing to do, and how unwise it always is to disturb the person who, if I may say so, is really the brains of the company.

Accordingly it had not been done, and unfortunately time was getting short, with the result that Barraclough, as I have said, was in one of his worst alarm clock moods. He had even tried to get me on the telephone the previous day, but even though one of his messages had eventually reached me, I had of course taken no notice of it. I never work out of business hours. Still, perhaps it was unfortunate, because Barraclough was certain that one of his frantic messages must have found me, and consequently would talk of nothing else. I tried to take advantage of the opportunity by pointing out that it was all Spencer's fault that I had been disturbed the day before, but the little man was beyond reason. He was merely in an insistent state of clamour that I should get on with a new advertisement for these people.

Well, if I was to have Barraclough's assistance in ejecting Spencer, I felt I had to humour him, and so—much though I hate working in a hurry—I sat down to try to oblige him by writing some new copy rapidly. There would, perhaps, just be time for Thomas to do some little thumb-nail sketch, but "I am afraid," I told Barraclough, "there will be no time to get the client's approval, nor for type-setting." Accidentally, this cheered him up, oddly enough. Type-setting, I should explain, is the process of making one block, not only of the drawing, but of the whole of the advertisement, words and all. It ensures that one can get the exact type one desires, and the words arranged as one wants. In cases, such as this one, where the same advertisement was to be used in several different papers, it made certain that all were the same. You could have copies—stereos, they are called—of the parent block sent to each paper.

Now I like to have my work type-set. I like to use unusual type, and now and then the papers—especially the smaller ones—cannot provide the exact variety I require. But it is expensive, and Barraclough, whose duty it was to answer any questions raised by the clients about the cost of producing their advertisements, loathed having to justify that expense, really because I believe that in his heart of hearts he was not convinced about the necessity.

In the case of Henriques, who kept a standard notice as to their drapery stores in the local press which circulated in the districts where they had a shop, he was particularly hard to convince. He used to say that the type-setting cost more than the advertisement, which was not true, unless you changed the advertisement every week, as I was always being urged to do.

Consequently my decision not to worry about typesetting for one week at any rate, gave little Barraclough immense pleasure. Considering how valuable that was to me, I set to work quite happily, determined to do my best. If Henriques were to be under the disadvantage of having local and probably bad arrangements of type, I must be particularly bright.

But it is not so easy to be bright in a hurry. We had been running for some while under the headline of 'Perfect Cut and Perfect Fit', and going on to talk about 'the glory that was Savile Row and the grandeur that was Bond Street', but I had had a lurking suspicion that I had been a little too classical. Still, it had served its turn, and the problem now was to think of another angle of approach. My first idea was 'London's Latest Lingerie for' Canterbury, Sittingbourne, or whatever the town was where the shops were—I never could remember. Anyhow, it would have to vary for each branch.

But on the whole I did not care for it. It was too condescending, and anyhow, I hate excessive alliteration. Then I coquetted with the notion of sex-appeal. Allure, just now, is the most popular line. 'Henriques' gowns will bring Him to you" or 'Henriques' dainty frills, will' do something which rhymed with frills. But I could think of nothing. 'Ills' would never do; you must never have anything ominous in an advertisement. 'Thrills' sounded promising, but somehow I could not get quite what I wanted. The real trouble was that I was not quite sure whether they wanted to emphasize their underwear department or their ready-made frocks and coats and things like that.

Eventually I thought I had better play for safety.

"And Now," I wrote. (Always a safe headline; you can introduce anything with it and it is invariably arresting.) "The New Hat." That would be bold in size, not quite so large as 'And Now'. On the whole I thought that those words ought not to be printed, but ought to look as if they had been dashed off, rather in a hurry, by a confident person. That would carry conviction. I sent them out to Thomas to do the lettering of them. It ought to please Barraclough, because he could make a charge for that which, though costing less to Henriques than the type-setting, would show us more profit.

"There is nothing," I went on happily with my copy—'nothing' in italics—"which will express the allure of your personality more surely than the New Hat. Messrs. Henriques in their wonderful showroom in"—wherever it was, I left a blank—"have an electrifying stock of the very latest models, direct from London and Paris." I underlined 'Paris'. Then I turned it round and underlined 'London'. Which, I wondered, created the most impression on the minds of farmers' wives and young women from offices and factories in the remoter districts of Kent? Paris might dazzle some of them. Others might be afraid of seeming to look too French. Perhaps, on the whole, this particular piece of copy was being directed mainly to the younger. Once the decision to stress Paris was made, the rest was easily completed. I was particularly pleased with 'electrifying'.

Just, however, as I finished, Barraclough came in to say he had been making enquiries after I had told Thomas to letter 'And Now, the New Hat', and that Henriques said they had rather a smaller stock of hats than usual. They wanted to get rid of an enormous consignment of cheap beads which one of their buyers had foolishly bought. Would we bring that in?

That is exactly the infuriating sort of thing which can happen to one. Here was all my work wasted—and incidentally Thomas's —and the Kent papers would have to go to press for another week with the same announcement as to Henriques. At any rate they could not say that it was anyone's fault but their own. If they had told us about the beads earlier I might have been able to do something about it. But anyhow, what can one say about beads?

At the last moment I had a brain wave. I merely put in 'Beads' instead of 'Hat'. With a very few alterations it did adequately well. I mean you cannot have everything all in a moment. Besides,

Thomas had already completed 'And Now'. Even so, we had to dispense with a formal approval from Henriques but, fortunately, they relied entirely on us. That we got the alteration made at all only shows how much more you can do for a client who gives you *carte blanche.*

CHAPTER FOUR

It has always been a weakness in my character that I overestimate the duration of human gratitude. I know very well that if you do anyone a good turn it is the greatest mistake possible to expect him to go on remembering it. But I do always hope that the effect will last for twenty-four hours.

That was the mistake I made about Barraclough. I hoped that seeing how much I had put myself out to oblige him, and what a convincing proof I had given him of how easy a collaborator I was, he would be prepared to back me up in getting rid of Spencer. But, as the sequel will show, I was quite wrong. Barraclough let me down completely, and apparently on the very ground which I should have thought would have prompted him to support me, a desire for peace and quiet.

I tackled the subject directly I arrived the next morning. No sooner had I hung my hat and coat up than I went straight in to his room, for although our offices were all very small we did manage to have a room for each of us—a cupboard would have been a more accurate description. I found Barraclough surrounded as usual by a mass of papers—the amount of stationery that man could collect was phenomenal.

As I came in, I noticed that he gave a slight start, and pushed away a page covered with figures on which he had been working. Why anyone should want to hide figures from me I could not make out; they mean nothing to me, a fact so well known to everyone, including Barraclough, that it ought to have made me realize at once that there was something very peculiar going on behind my back. At the time I merely thought that I had disturbed him when he was engaged on some work of his own during office hours. Personally I should not have minded if he had been, but Barraclough was always the slave of his conscience and liked to pretend that he never had a moment to spare. But I ought to have been more suspicious. I wish I had been; it would have given me firmer ground from which to press my point in the meeting which I was just about to summon.

The first check came from Barraclough. He actually demurred at my proposition to call a company conference that afternoon. He sat there chewing the end of his sandy moustache—an irritating habit—and pointedly looking at the piles of accounts and papers on his table. I must admit that I had forgotten that it was the day on which he sent out the monthly accounts.

"But what do you want to talk about, Nicholas? Wouldn't it wait for a day or so? I'm frightfully busy just now."

"I have never known you be anything else. Your industry, you know---"

That made him smile a bit.

"Well, but what about? A conference, you know," he made a feeble joke, "sounds as if we were prime ministers or foreign secretaries. Oughtn't we to go to the Carlton to hold it?"

I did my best to smile.

"Well, perhaps conference was the wrong word. I believe you call it a general meeting."

That touched him on his secretarial side. He began to quote the Company's Act—as if we were going to let ourselves be interfered with by little things like Acts of Parliament. So far as I could make out you could not hold a meeting without some long notice —I think he said fourteen full days. I wonder what the difference is between a full day and an empty day? However, that is not the point.

"But, good heavens," I went on, "do you really mean to say that we can't take any important steps ever without giving ourselves a fortnight's warning about it? Why, the business could be ruined in less than that. May very well be ruined, so far as I can see," I added, rather neatly putting the idea into his mind.

Barraclough smiled, "We are not tied up with red tape quite so badly as that. The directors can make decisions at any time, and as all the shareholders are directors, it comes to the same thing."

"Well, then, that's what I want. A Board Meeting."

"Oh," Barraclough looked at me rather hard. "You said a general meeting."

"Well, a general meeting of the Board for the purpose of——"

"Yes, for the purpose of what, Nicholas?"

Now that it had come to the moment when I must convince Barraclough of the necessity of voting Spencer off the Board, I hesitated for a second, and during that second, unfortunately, Spencer came in. My chance of talking Barraclough over quietly first had gone. Directly he saw Paul open the door, he said quickly: "Nicholas wants a Board Meeting this afternoon."

"Why not now?"

As a matter of fact Spencer's suggestion rather rushed me; I had not fully thought out what I wanted to say; but I was not going to admit that. At first I thought that Barraclough was going to get the postponement for me. He glanced almost wistfully at the papers on his desk, and was just going to insist, I believe, on getting them out of the way, when Spencer cut in and answered his thought.

"You will have just as much on your desk this afternoon; you know you will. And I have got an appointment at three o'clock which may take the rest of the afternoon and another to-morrow.

So it's now or never, or at any rate much later. Fire ahead, Nicholas."

Thus crudely abjured, I had to begin at once. I do like things done formally and here we were, all standing about without an agenda or any proper organization—with the atmosphere all wrong. However, I did my best. I pointed out that the business was not increasing. In fact that profits were going steadily down, I believed. No doubt the books of the company would show that best. That was so well-known that neither of them could possibly contest that.

"And why?" I went on rhetorically.

"I wouldn't like to tell you, Nicholas," murmured Spencer. "Give me a match." It was so like him to interrupt just as I was getting into my stride. Also I had not got a match and there was delay and confusion while Spencer yelled to the outer office for Thomas to bring him one. That man was never happy unless he had involved every one in his own confusion.

When quiet was restored, I went on.

"Because the directors—or if you force me to put it that way— because I am always being disturbed from getting on with what is important. In a minor way you have just had a perfect example. In a major way I would instance this Greystone---"

"Greyfields," put in Barraclough.

"Greyfields Canning affair."

Spencer knocked the ash off his cigarette with elaborate ease.

"So an attempt to get business is called 'a disturbance'. Well, we live and learn."

"Some of us only live," I snapped out. "Not an attempt to get business. A wild cat scheme on which the productive side of the business was asked to take a hand very prematurely to put the best possible construction on it."

"And what do you propose?" Spencer's voice was icy.

Now that the decisive moment was come, I felt only the faintest throb of excitement.

"I propose," I said, slowly and quietly, to show that I had made up my mind after long consideration, "much as I regret it, that since you are the cause of the disturbance, that you cease to be a member of the Board."

An ironic bow from Spencer.

"I shall do myself the honour of opposing that."

I turned towards Barraclough and appealed to him. Surely I could count on his common sense? To my intense irritation he was showing a complete lack of any knowledge of the importance of the occasion. He was actually checking the addition of a column of figures. I had to ask him twice how he would vote. His reply was amazing.

"There now, I've lost count. Vote? I? Oh, I shan't vote." And with that he plunged back into his books.

Spencer, whose sense of humour is never appropriate, positively grinned.

"And now I shall do myself the honour to propose that Nicholas ceases to be a member of the Board." (The cheek of using my Christian name in the circumstances!) "I may, I think, take it that Nicholas opposes that. And you, Barraclough, are you voting? I thought not, but you might say 'No' instead of grunting."

"Wait a minute, I believe I am the chairman of this company. So, with my casting vote I declare the motion carried."

"What, the one I proposed, Nicholas? You surprise me."

"And eight are fourteen. Miss Wyndham is getting most careless. This company has no chairman. We agreed to that long ago in order to prevent this."

"Your grammar!" interjected Spencer.

"Then I propose that I be chairman," I went on, desperately trying to restore sense.

"So do I, only that I substitute myself. And Barraclough can propose himself. And there we are. How long has this farce got to go on? Can't you stop him, Barraclough?"

"In a way, yes. All these proposals are beside the point. We all have service agreements with the company. Even if I did vote either of you off the Board, you could still draw a third of the profits, if any. That's the only reason I did not agree to both your resolutions."

Spencer looked at me.

"I believe that is the first joke our friend has ever made."

"It was not a joke. Latimer is right over one thing. If you two do not stop quarrelling there will not only be no profits to divide, but we shall soon have to wind up. We must have peace and quiet internally. The position of the company is very poor—only I can never get either of you to realize it."

"Precisely, and that is why I give you a further chance to support me. It would be cheaper for this company to pay Spencer his share for nothing than to have him upsetting me."

It was a home thrust, and however much he might pretend to be amused, Spencer knew quite well that it was. As for Barraclough, for a hopeful moment I thought he was going to say 'yes'. He got up from the table and looked out of the window while both of us waited, I with the hopefulness born of common sense, Spencer buoyed up by his innate optimism and conceit.

Eventually the third member of our trio turned back.

"I vote for---" he began, and then he paused, "neither motion."

There was no denying it was an anticlimax and a considerable disappointment to me.

"And now," went on Barraclough's voice, "let me seriously recommend both of you to stop this. Especially you, Latimer." I suppose he chose me because one always instinctively appeals to the most rational person; otherwise, of course, the appeal was much more needed by Spencer. "We must stop fighting each other. Now, as a beginning, can't I induce you to consider again the question of this canning company? Really, you know, there is something in it."

"There is nothing whatever. I should very much like to think that there was, just to show you how reasonable I am. But really it is so wildly preposterous. Why, you wouldn't consent to work out all those figures yourself, now, would you?"

Barraclough rather staggered me by saying that he would, but at the time I did not believe him.

"Well, perhaps you have the time. In any case, the affair has about reached your stage of the work. What neither of you seem able to see is that it is nowhere near so far advanced as to concern me."

"And never will if you can help it. It's an extraordinary thing"—this was one of Spencer's usual openings to something particularly rude—"but it never does reach Nicholas's turn to do a job of work."

"I had hoped to do a good one this morning," I retorted, "but unfortunately I have been prevented."

With that I closed an interview which was clearly going to produce no valuable results, and from which I had hoped to get so much.

But at least it had had one advantage. I had found out that by some means, fair or foul, I must get rid of Paul Spencer. Really, I cared very little what those means were. Whatever was easiest would be best.

CHAPTER FIVE

I t is curious how one's mind, if you let it pursue a train of thought unchecked, will unconsciously arrive at conclusions and present them to yourself almost as a *fait accompli,* although consciously you have not been considering them at all.

Let me explain that general statement by the particular example of this actual case. When I said to myself that I would get rid of Spencer by any means, fair or foul, I had nothing very definite in my thoughts. I had tried one quite fair method. I intended to try others if I could think of them. But so far as foul was concerned, I had nothing definite in my thoughts. I merely felt that if an opportunity to do a trick, which in normal circumstances I should consider beneath me, were thrust under my nose, I should find it hard to resist. But such is the vigour of my intellect when once it has been aroused, that before I knew where I was, I was turning over in my brain, not the question of whether I should get rid of Spencer by physical means, but the best and safest way of so doing.

I must admit that it was rather a shock to me. The idea came to me so suddenly, so fully fledged, that I was hardly prepared for it. But once it was present in my thoughts, I was bound to see the advantages of it. Not that I should employ it until there was no other course open—it was only to be used as a last resort. Still, just in case that last resort should be necessary, it would be wise to consider the question, since whatever else you may say about murder—I believe in calling a spade a spade—it isn't easy.

Of course, in a crude way, it is perfectly simple. Any one can buy a knife and stick it in someone else's back. It is merely a question of courage. But I am too much of an artist to do that. I had no intention of—to use a vulgar phrase—swinging for Spencer. Frankly, he was not worth it.

For the moment therefore, I just let the idea lie in my mind. In due course some simple but ingenious thought would, I had no doubt, occur to me. I find that all my best inspirations come by just letting an idea, perhaps merely a desire for an idea, lie apparently idle in my brain until at the right moment, after being to external appearances dismissed from my thoughts, the really original notion suddenly springs up fully formed, apparently from nowhere. That was one of the things both my co-directors could never understand. They were always expecting me to go on thinking continuously over some problem until a solution was reached. A foolish method. The best solutions come as spontaneous inspirations.

I was therefore quite happy to forget, apparently, all about Spencer—I may even have deceived him into a sense of false security by my inaction—especially as about this time a really important piece of work came our way.

It was introduced, I need hardly say, by me.

I had been spending an interesting and rather instructive day at the Drug and Allied Trades Exhibition. Spencer, of course, said I was wasting time by going there, but that merely displayed his ignorance. How am I to write good copy, to get new ideas, to keep my brain fresh, if I do not see the work which other people are doing, the way in which they decorate their stands at such an exhibition for instance—in short, if I do not keep in touch with modern sales methods?

I think Spencer's criticism was based on the fact that I sometimes spend a few minutes in looking at the latest novelties which attract me and which I might find suitable for my personal use, but after all, if a thing compels my attention, it probably asserts the same influence on other people, and I ought to find out what the sales point is which has caused the attraction.

Something—I forget what—had called itself to my notice that day and I had been discussing it with someone on the stand and telling him that the merits of the product fully justified extensive advertising. He must have had some control of the business because he demurred as to the expense. He had not, he said, unlimited capital. In, I must admit, a rather lordly way, I told him that we could often arrange that. I gave him our card. After all, if NeO-aD is never to nod, one must take every opportunity, however unlikely.

I might have talked to him longer, but that a curious-looking man came up and apparently wished to talk to the stallholder. I did not realize then, as I did later, that he had been standing there for some time, but when I did become aware of his presence, I moved off at once. I had sown the seed for what it was worth—nothing, as it happened, but one must try—and I had no desire to run the risk of being a bore by pressing myself and our claims on him further. That sort of mistake I leave to Spencer.

Accordingly I stepped back, and, true to my policy of finding out what type of man was attracted by any particular thing, I studied the strange individual who was now talking to the stallholder. He was, as I have said, a curious-looking man, probably foreign, but I found it hard to place his nationality. Dark, rather swarthy, with little beady black eyes, and a chin faintly blue. I at first put him down as a Frenchman, save that no Frenchman could have worn a tie whose colour scheme was such an offence. I was wondering if he might be Italian, rather than Portuguese, when I saw that he had noticed that I was still there, and anxious not to be guilty of a breach of good manners, I wandered off. As a matter of fact I had seen a refreshment room and was tired after a heavy day. Tea would be pleasant, and well-earned.

I had hardly sat down at a rather depressing little table—it was artistically wrong in that it was trying to be too perfect, and anyhow I hate imitation flowers—when the little man came in.

He looked round the room until he saw me and then, to my surprise, came straight up to me.

"Ah, monsieur"—a low bow, rather embarrassing in a public place—"your glove."

It is extremely irritating to lose one glove, almost worse than losing a pair. I must have laid it down on the stall when I got out my business card. Naturally I thanked him politely. But I suppose I must have been more than usually civil to him as he was a foreigner. At any rate I impressed him prodigiously. Considering how valuable a client I think he is going to be to us, it only shows how wise casual politeness is.

But I anticipate.

At the time he had no more idea of my line of business than I had of his. In fact I discovered something about his first. He had, naturally enough I suppose, sat down beside me, and I felt that I ought to say something, if only to prove that the English are not so frigid as they are alleged to be.

"You will pardon the question, but I was wondering just now—I hope you will not think me inquisitive, but do you by any chance come from Italy?"

"From Italy?" His eyes flashed. "Monsieur, you should be more careful. The Italians———" he flashed off suddenly into a stream of comments in his own language. Fortunately no one could understand them, but even so, coupled with his yellow and magenta tie and black suit, his elaborate bow, and his grey suede shoes, he attracted a considerable amount of attention. I began to think that I had better find an excuse to leave, but there was my tea and anyhow, apparently, I had annoyed him. I felt I had to stay. I am glad now that I did.

Eventually he began to calm down.

"Monsieur, monsieur, you should not mention Italy to me. A bas, Mussolini! I am"—he thumped his chest dramatically—"Rrumanian." (Well, he pronounced it like that.) "M. Tonescu," he added, waving a card towards my plate with a dramatic gesture of so sweeping a nature, that he planted it firmly in a chocolate fancy cake. It stuck in it, like one of the notices at a cocktail party, describing which kind of sandwich is which.

"Ah, pardon, monsieur." With more restraint he presented me with another.

I have never quite known what I ought to have done about the first one. Eventually, when we left, it was still embedded in the sticky mess, and I had not the courage to mention it to the waitress, so that I still feel that I owe that restaurant the price of a chocolate cake.

However, at the moment, I was more engaged in restoring peace. I apologized for my error. The English were always so ignorant, I pleaded. I went on to hope that he was enjoying his stay in England.

"Alas! Monsieur, I have no time for enjoyment. I am here on business. There must be no pleasure till that is done. I have an invention—oh! so excellent!—which I and my friends intend to place on the market here, for it is in this country that the great sales"—his emphasis of 'great' was positively inspiring—"are made. Ah, of a certainty, I see a great future for us. Everything is ready. We have the manufacture plans abroad, we have the shipping arranged, it needs only but two things."

"And those are?" I asked. I had already begun to see a chance for NeO-aD. You never know when business will not crop up.

"Firstly the capital. That is easy. We have that nearly arranged. We are not like your friend down there"—he waved a hand in the direction where I had left my glove. "The restriction on export of the lei—our Rumanian unit of coinage, monsieur—it has caused a little trouble, but that is nearly overcome. Besides, we need here only enough to cover the—how do you call them?—the selling costs. That will be easy. In six months, it will be done and there will be great profits for all of us. And while that arranges itself, I study the second thing. Your British sales methods. It will not do, monsieur, to present my great invention to this country as I would in Rumania. No, no."

Of course, by now I was quite sure that there was a chance for us. Here was a point of view that was so sensible. He was perfectly right. Despite the fluency with which he spoke English, there was the accent—a charming sing-song lilt which made the slight variations in the stress of the words a pleasure to listen to. Above all, there were the eccentricities of dress. He would be certain if he carried out his own invention to offend English taste in some way. Here, clearly, was an opportunity where we could help. I took the liberty of expressing my admiration for his acumen in foreseeing the difficulties.

"Curiously enough," I went on, "I believe I might be able to help you."

"You, monsieur? But I thought there was a fate which had made me pick up your glove! But how would you help? I heard you talking just now of finance—you will pardon the liberty, but I could not avoid. There is no need—or at least, very little need—of finance."

"The company of which I am the chairman" (well, I ought to be and it sounded more authoritative) "has made a special study of modern sales methods. We are not haphazard. Our methods are the most up-to-date and scientific possible. We are capable of advising you as to everything connected with the subject, from the preparation of wrappers for your boxes, or containers for your packages whatever it may be, through all the complicated processes of catalogues, literature to the trade and so on, right up to the preparation of press advertising. In short, we know how to approach the buyers of every trade as well as the public."

My heart warmed at the thought. I had always wanted to be in from the very start at the birth of a new product. I could see, too, that I had made a definite impression on the mind of Tonescu.

"So.... Indeed.... Then clearly this is fated! Yes, you shall help me with my great invention."

I began to get a little cautious. After all, it was a very definite rule of NeO-aD that no client should be accepted without the consent of all three directors. Barraclough had originally wanted it for some financial reason or another and I had backed him up so as to retain real control. But though of course the rule had never been directed against me, still, perhaps it would be as well to humour Barraclough. Besides, I was always a stickler for the proprieties.

"I hope so, I am sure. But Monsieur Tonescu, I must get my colleagues' consent before we begin to act."

"Your colleagues? Ah, yes. There are many?"

"Two."

"But you are the chairman?"

"Yes, actually. Though not in name. Of course they are really subordinates of mine, but I prefer to work with them as fellow directors of the company. I am sure you understand."

"But perfectly. And what are their particular departments?"

"One of them is supposed to get the business—though in this case"—I gave a little laugh—"I seem to be doing that. The other is concerned with finance."

The mention of Barraclough's activities hardly seemed to interest Tonescu.

"Ah, yes, finance. But that, I told you, is all arranged. I think my friends would not consent to part with any of their share in my invention."

Up to that moment, as a matter of fact, I had not considered the idea that we wanted to do anything of the kind, nor had I, so far as I could remember, suggested anything of the sort. Perhaps M. Tonescu's understanding of English, though it appeared to be perfect, had betrayed him for once. In any case I should not pursue that point further at the moment. I should content myself with bearing it in mind. I turned the conversation, therefore, to a slightly different angle of the same topic.

"But you have not yet told me what your invention is."

Tonescu looked round rather in the manner of a stage conspirator.

"Here I would hardly like to say—not in detail. One does not know what ears overhear one. I will just whisper to you very quietly."

Really the scene must have been slightly ridiculous. Whispering in public is always absurd, but particularly so when the man who is imparting confidences is as flamboyant and theatrical as Tonescu. Nor could I really see why he could not say openly of what type his invention was. The details of the process perhaps should have been given in confidence, but I had not asked him for anything of that kind, nor probably would it have conveyed any meaning to me if he had. However, if that was Tonescu's way of doing things, I had to put up with it.

There seemed to be nothing particularly secret about his communication, though that his invention, if it really worked, was a good one, I had no doubt. He claimed to have discovered a process by which glass would not become clouded by steam or heat and which would cause water to run off it quickly. Tonescu was all for praising its value for the looking-glasses of bathrooms. It just shows how the foreign mind can get lost as to the habits of another country. Tonescu, coming from Rumania, a country where I believe there are practically no bathrooms, had heard British habits of cleanliness spoken of so often that he considered anything that could be used in connection with washing, to be all important. As for its obvious principal use, for the windscreens of cars, I doubt if he had ever thought of it!

CHAPTER SIX

"Butreally, Nicholas, you know it's preposterous."

That was the way, if you please, in which Barraclough received my news. As for Spencer, he just sat there grinning sardonically. I could see that he was determined to disapprove. In fact I expected him to be in opposition, but for the present, Barraclough was doing his work for him. There was no need for Spencer to take any action as yet.

So far as Barraclough was concerned, I was not really surprised, either. He had always a kind of automatic resistance to any new idea, bred simply by his natural timidity. He was afraid, that was all it was. His first reaction to anything was always to see the difficulties; give him time in which to accustom himself to the new idea and he would come round. Meanwhile I had to humour him by taking his objections seriously and meeting them squarely with logic.

"It is a little startling, I admit. One does not often get such a chance thrown at one so easily, I know. Still, even as to that, I think I may say that I acted with vigour. We should not have got this opportunity if I had not made it."

"I wonder," broke in Spencer. "Oh, not what you mean,

Nicholas. I am not implying that you did not do your best, but I wonder why the opportunity fell so pat. Quite sure this man, Tonescu, was not aware all the time who you were? Is it possible that he overheard your gossip with this fellow on the stall?"

I think it was the word 'gossip' which annoyed me. It was not the first time that Spencer had implied that my conversations with prospective clients were mere idle chatter, and that I said more to them than I should. I was sure that in fact Tonescu had had no idea who I was when he returned me my glove; therefore any discussion as to the possibility of his having known, was a mere waste of time. But if once I admitted that I had been talking about NeO-aD while Tonescu was within a hundred yards, I should never convince either of my co-directors of the fact. So I decided quite simply—and I think quite wisely—to suppress the incident.

I hardly worried to reply to Spencer. Instead, I turned to Barraclough and asked him for his reasons for pouring cold water on the whole affair.

"It's like this. Here is a process which every motor company in the world has been searching for. Just think of the sum in cash down that Morris or Austin or Ford would give for the sole rights to use such a patent. For that matter, think how much research has gone on by every company that makes cars—and they can afford to employ the ablest men—to find out just such a thing. And then you arrive with a man you pick up casually at the Allied Drug Trades Exhibition---"

"I did not 'pick him up'. I object to the phrase."

"Well, word it that you hooked him with a cast baited with one glove."

This, I need hardly say, was Spencer's flippant intrusion. I treated it as it deserved, by ignoring it while Barraclough went on as if neither of us had spoken.

"—who announces that he has this invention and thinks that it might be useful in bathrooms—who is proposing to market it in this country with every expectation of making handsome profits, but without being aware of its principal and most obvious use. To my mind it is too ingenuous."

"Especially when you add the appearance of Nicholas's friend."

Spencer's interruption gave me my clue. It is very remarkable how a fool will always destroy the case he is trying to make.

"But that is exactly the proof! Here you have a man who is completely ignorant of the world. The roads in Rumania are very bad, I believe. Probably they very rarely see a car———"

"I should think it is far more likely that they never see a bath." (Spencer again.)

"I see no reason why either of you should be rude to the Rumanians," Barraclough went on. "Latimer's story certainly shows that they know all about baths, or at any rate about English habits, and everybody knows about cars and the difficulty of driving in the rain."

"No. That's exactly it. Everybody does not know about the difficulty of driving in the rain, because everybody is not cursed with the English climate. In many places it is either fine and you can drive or it is wet and the roads become impassable. Rumania is probably one of them."

"Just as a pure question of fact, Nicholas, do you know anything about the climate of Rumania? I mean, do you know that the roads there are really impassable in wet weather for the cars which you have just told us are not there?"

A preposterous question, and so like Spencer. Why should I have any special knowledge on such a subject, and why should he twist my words round so?

"Only what every schoolboy knows," I answered.

"And that is?"

"What I have just said."

"You must have been to a very remarkable school where they give you very unusual, but very practical, information."

"That's right. Now start sneering. Even if you were at a better-known public school, there is no need to be offensive."

"Stop it, both of you." I had never known Barraclough be so firm before. "We are discussing the question of what action to take about Tonescu and his invention. Not your old school ties. Nor even the climate of Rumania."

"Quite right. Do bring Nicholas back to the point."

"I like that. I was just proving to you why your suggestion that Tonescu must have known all about the advantages of his invention for driving in rain was not certain, when Spencer pulled the conversation round to the subject of schools."

Very offensively Barraclough sighed and with laboured reticence returned to Tonescu.

"Well," he admitted with obvious reluctance, "Latimer complains that I have poured cold water on his project. I do not think that that is true. I think that I have only called your attention to the fact that a little obvious caution is necessary before we rush blindfold towards associating ourselves with an invention which may not prove to be all that it is supposed to be—of which quite frankly I have considerable doubts."

I decided to see what he wanted. Very often Barraclough's bark was worse than his bite. He might only require quite simple precautions.

"Exactly what do you mean?" I asked.

"First I suggest that we have a look at this compound of his and test it out ourselves."

I nodded. There could be no harm in that.

"In the second place, I should only accept orders for work after taking considerable financial precautions."

"You mean?"

"Payment in advance."

I jumped up at that.

"A very ingenious way of killing the whole thing. No one would accept such an insult."

"Why not?" went on Barraclough. "If he is as ignorant of English habits as you say, you might induce him to believe that it was the normal practice. In point of fact I have heard of its being done. If that cannot be arranged—and you may shake your head as much as you like, Latimer, I think it could—you might point out that his financial backing is abroad and that he himself spoke of the difficulty of exporting capital. Incidentally I am going to see if I can find out if that statement is right or not."

"I think that even Nicholas must admit that if that point of view is put properly to Tonescu, he must see that it is quite reasonable."

"I should think it most unlikely. You see I have seen Tonescu. You have not. I should say that he was thoroughly temperamental."

"He can be as temperamental as he likes, but I agree with Barraclough. Without those two safeguards I recommend that we don't touch the thing with the end of a very long barge pole."

"In other words you both want to kill the plan—solely because I suggested it."

"Don't be childish," Spencer had the impertinence to say. I shall not forget that insult, nor shall I forgive the opposition that he was making solely on personal grounds. Once more, however, Barraclough attempted to pour oil on the troubled waters, and as usual merely succeeded in making things worse. Eventually, however, after a discussion of an appalling length—all our conferences at NeO-aD were apt to be protracted—I induced them to consider the proposed business favourably and consented that we should investigate it fully, and that possible financial safeguards should be carefully explored, a watering down of Barraclough's original inflexible attitude.

And that was all the gratitude I got for bringing in this valuable piece of business! Truly, as I said at the start of these notes, there is a limit to the extent to which the folly of any man can be allowed to ruin a business. My only doubt is whether I ought not to include Barraclough as well as Spencer. But no, Spencer is the real stumbling-block. I must never forget for a minute that it is Spencer who must go.

But as if ingratitude was not enough, I was positively subjected to insult. Spencer had the impertinence to complain that I was interfering in his domain by introducing a client!

"Well," I said, "if you don't do your work, someone has to do it for you."

"The *tu quoque* is exactly what I want to bring out when I bring work in. You neglect your own work, which is production, and you would be the first to make an outcry if I started to do it for you, but you have no hesitation in taking on something you know nothing about and forcing both Barraclough and me to dance to your piping."

"Back to that canning thing again!"

"Yes. Back to Greyfields. We shall want to do so sometime."

"I doubt it. But anyhow that is no reason why I should not introduce Tonescu."

"None—provided that Greyfields is not neglected. But I only wish to point out that if I do not complain at your intrusion, you must not complain if I enter your province."

I could afford a superior smile.

"I think you will find it rather a difficult province to enter—for the amateur."

For once Spencer's pretense of indifference to whatever I might say gave way. He was frequently bad-tempered, but never before had I been able to make him lose control of himself by a direct statement. I suppose it was the truth that rankled so bitterly. He leapt to his feet and upset a table in so doing. For a moment I thought he was going to strike me, but eventually he contented himself with mere vulgar abuse before he crashed back into his own room and slammed the door with a resounding bang.

Even if there is a slight lack of harmony amongst us, Spencer should not advertise the fact to Thomas and Miss Wyndham and the office boys.

If this goes on much longer it will be a question merely of method as to how I eliminate Spencer. I wonder now if I could so arrange things that suspicion would fall upon Barraclough? Not perhaps to so great an extent as to cause him to be actually convicted, but sufficient to frighten him. Perhaps on the whole, though, it would not do. Apart from being rather difficult to arrange, it would be a nuisance to have Barraclough away from the office. I mean, someone in authority—even if only with limited authority—must be available to answer the telephone or deal with the unexpected visit of a client.

Besides, Barraclough is very useful in dealing with press representatives, those ceaseless intruders in an advertising agency's office.

No, though I am more and more coming to the conclusion that Spencer must die—and die soon—I think I shall leave Barraclough out of it.

CHAPTER SEVEN

The curse of an advertising agency and, at the same time, the charm, because of its variety, is the impossibility of concentrating on one thing.

It would seem natural that having before us this extremely interesting problem of Tonescu, we should have been thinking of that to the exclusion of everything else. But such a course was quite out of the question. There was always routine work to do.

You see, advertising, to be of any value, must have continuity, and only a very few of the really big spenders are able to keep up a continuous campaign to the public. That they profit by it is certain, but it is more than a small business can be expected to contemplate. So, now and again, even if the work is well done, the sales do not immediately respond, and really a company should work its finances with that as a possible danger—an improbable one of course, and one which scientific methods of preliminary research, such as we used when the client would permit it, should almost entirely obviate. Still, small businesses must be cautious, and besides, we have to recommend them to be. *We* cannot afford bad debts!

But while continuous advertising to the public is an ideal not always obtainable, except to a limited public, such as Henriques' announcements in the Kentish press, to the trade it is not only possible, but essential. That really is why trade papers prosper, and also why, unfortunately, they are so numerous. There is no trade which is not catered for by at least two papers, except, I believe, that the Undertakers have only one.

But as for some of the others, they abound. Motoring, medicine, and drapery are the three biggest sections. Motoring papers of course go, not only to the trade—they are bought also by that part of the public which is especially interested. The same may be said of medicine—who, by the way, may be slightly hurt at being referred to as 'trade'. I mean no insult. We always classified them as such in a rather comprehensive way. But because there were so many, I had got Barraclough to draw up rather a valuable summary of facts about all such papers. He became peculiarly interested in the medical ones. I believe he had notes on over a hundred journals of that sort.

Now the real point of an announcement in a trade journal is simply that your name shall appear—if possible, prominently. I have always considered that it mattered very little what you said in them, especially in those which were trade and trade only, such as the *Grocer's Gazette* or the *Baker and Confectioner*. The same would not be quite true of the *British Medical Journal* or the *Autocar*. But I could never get Spencer to see my point as to the purely trade papers, and of course he encouraged the client. Clients like to see something different every week. I never could be sure why. I think partly natural perversity, because they knew it annoyed me, and partly desire to see how much work they could get out of me for nothing.

I am, of course, thinking of a particular client; a personal friend of Spencer's and a personal enemy of mine. He had some cure, I expect a quite inefficient cure, for influenza, which he insisted, contrary to my advice, in advertising weekly in small spaces in the *Chemist and Druggist* and in that alone. Now I have not a word to say against the *Chemist and Druggist,* but it is not a complete campaign. I mean, you might get Flukil on to the shelves of every chemist in Great Britain—in fact probably had—but you did not get it off those shelves and into the hands of the public just by using that. It was not fair on the paper. Moreover, it was one of the very few journals who had strict conscientious objections to paying commission to agents—I never could understand their point of view—and so we had to make a special charge to Flukil.

Naturally that gave Spencer's friend an opportunity to say that we cost him something—I believe Spencer egged him on—and he took it out of us by insisting on having different copy each week.

Each week! For the first six weeks or so I found it quite easy, but when I suggested that we should now return to the original and so go on in a cycle, I was met with a blank refusal. So, having already said the six best things about it, I was forced to go on saying the second best things, and after that the third, and so on. Naturally they were not so good, and then Flukil—I never could remember that man's name—began to complain. Personally I should have washed the whole thing out, but Spencer, who never could see how much of my brains he used up on trivialities, insisted on my obliging his friend. What makes me particularly certain that Spencer was behind Flukil's complaints, was that when I absolutely refused to produce something new, or when I simply had no time to deal with it, Barraclough put in some nonsense of his own, and Flukil always rang me up and congratulated me on the wording. Barraclough's stuff, I need hardly say, was so hopeless that it must have been a deliberate plot.

I only give this just as one example of what was constantly happening to pull me back from the heights and keep me tied down and prevented from soaring.

While, then, I was struggling to find the two hundred and sixty-ninth thing (or thereabouts) to say about Flukil, and was deciding to adopt 'Summer Colds' as a headline, I could not be concentrating on Tonescu as I should. The point I wanted to get down to was what to call the substance.

It was, I gathered, something that you could yourself rub on to glass, wherever you liked, quite simply. A good name I felt was all important. It should suggest to your mind at once that wind-screen wipers were unnecessary, that you would be able to see clearly, however heavy the rain. That is to say, that is what the name should imply so far as cars were concerned. As to mirrors, something that suggested that no mist would form on them, was what was wanted. The trouble was to get one word to imply both. I mean things like 'Clerevue' or 'Exrain' would imply the first and 'Nevcloud' or 'Alclear' the second. Perhaps 'Everclear' would do both. But it hardly included the connection with glass.

I was just, I felt, on the verge of a really good idea, when the telephone bell rang and I found myself once more distracted by an absurd and trivial interruption. Henriques, if you please, had the impertinence to be dissatisfied with the advertisement we had put in for them about beads! They complained that so far as they could make out it had sold no beads at all.

"But what do you expect," I somewhat incautiously began to answer. Before I had time to explain my point old Henriques himself interrupted me.

"We expect, Mr. Latimer, that when we pay for space in a large number of papers and allow you to put in whatever you please, that the effect will be an increase in sales. That is what we expect, and I think it is well that you should know it. Not, as has happened in this case according to the figures before me from each of our branches, an instantaneous and proportionately substantial decrease."

"You did not give me time to finish. Of course, ultimately, that not only will be what you expect, but what I am sure will happen. But you forget the time factor. I was going to say, 'But what do you expect in four days?' The increase in sales, you know, cannot be instantaneous. Now, if you persevere with that advertisement for another six weeks, I am sure---"

"Six weeks! At the present rate of decrease our sales will be a minus quantity in less than a month."

I forbore from pressing the mathematical point. A month may be four weeks or five. Clearly Henriques was not thinking accurately. Besides, before I had time to say anything he went on:

"No, I absolutely refuse to have that nonsense repeated. Let me read one phrase of it to you. 'The very latest models from London and from Paris'. Apart from the fact that it sounds like accidental blank verse, no one ever talks about models in connection with beads. Besides, our windows are plastered with 'Buy British', and you make our advertisements talk about Paris! Several customers have made some very acid comments on it and the people from whom we bought the beads are turning very nasty about it."

"Where did you get them from?"

"An English house. But where they were made, as a matter of fact, I have no idea. That is exactly what makes it so very awkward. I rather suspect that they are, in fact, Japanese."

"I see. I wish I had known all this."

"So do I. And I go further. I think you ought to have found it out before you rushed into print recklessly."

Now, as a matter of fact, it was Henriques' own insistence at the last moment, coupled with Barraclough's officious telephoning to find out whether they liked 'And Now—The New Hat' which had caused me to make any mention of beads at all. I tried to suggest this tactfully to Henriques, but it was no good. He was determined to judge merely by results, and by results of such a short period too—although there was some substance in his point about country of origin. Seeing therefore that logic would be wasted upon him, I determined to appease him by offering to put in whatever he liked. I mean of course whatever selling point he liked. I had no intention of letting him actually write the wording.

Unfortunately, however, he misunderstood me and I had to listen to another lecture.

"Oh, so now I am to write the advertisement, am I? Would you mind telling me what advantage we get from employing you? First we leave it to you, give you a free hand and let you behave exactly as you wish. That was what you asked for and what we granted, and now at the first breath of criticism—and criticism founded on facts, mind you—you calmly suggest that we should do the work, while you confine yourselves to taking the commission."

Now dealing with angry clients is not really my department. It is Spencer's. It was entirely wrong that Henriques should have been put through to me at all. For that Miss Wyndham was to blame. She should have seen to it that I was not worried, but as Barraclough was saying only a day or so before, that girl was getting thoroughly careless. It is my view that she has fallen in love with Thomas. Of course, if she has, she will be quite useless and we had better sack them both at once.

However, there it was. Henriques had been put on to me and I had to do my best to calm him down. Before I was quite aware what I was doing, I had foolishly promised to do all sorts of things for him. So far as I can make out, for the future, Henriques will be as bad a curse as Flukil, and between the two of them I shall get no peace, no time to produce constructive ideas at all. Besides, there was a very definite threat that if he did not get results and get them quickly, Henriques would go elsewhere. I hate being judged by results, especially over a short space of time; it is not fair; besides, it makes me nervous, and so I do not do myself justice. It would never do to lose Henriques. They were a very useful piece of bread and butter.

No sooner was the telephone conversation over (and my arm was aching by the time it was), than I went to the outer office to explain her mistake to Miss Wyndham. But it was not my lucky day. She was almost insolent and quite impenitent.

"Well, Mr. Latimer, what was I to do? Mr. Spencer was out and Mr. Barraclough had had about as much of Mr. Henriques as he could stand. He said that it was your copy and he thought you ought to defend it."

"That will do, Miss Wyndham. Please understand in future that clients are not to be put on to me."

I am glad to say that Miss Wyndham realized that she had been put in her place. As I went out I saw that one of the boys whose duty it was to collect voucher copies of the papers and run messages generally, was grinning at her discomfiture. As I shut the door behind me, I fancy I heard Thomas taking it out of the boy. Now why should Thomas worry to interfere with what is not his business? I am getting more and more suspicious that he and Miss Wyndham are becoming far too close allies.

CHAPTER EIGHT

I know nothing more fascinating than to watch the effect of the unusual on the commonplace, and of this Tonescu has afforded me a most interesting example. I have very much enjoyed watching the reactions to him of Spencer, a typical, florid, unthinking, insular Englishman, and of the reticent, dry, cautious Barraclough, who must certainly have some Scottish blood in him. But the chance that I was in the outer office when Tonescu arrived, gave me the opportunity of observing in addition, the attitude of two ordinary English people, namely Miss Wyndham and Thomas. Tonescu was something of a class they had never had to do with previously.

Miss Wyndham's face was an absolute sight. At any time she has a slightly surprised expression, due, I think, more to her protruding teeth and receding chin than to the fact that she is startled, although her brain is so limited that anything which is the slightest trifle out of the ordinary, does amaze her. Whenever I see a newspaper announcing some ordinary fact as a 'surprise' or a 'sensation', I always picture Miss Wyndham standing with her mouth open, showing those rabbit-like teeth and peering over her pince-nez and saying "Fancy! Well I never!" in awestruck tones.

As for Tonescu, his arrival made her completely dumb, especially as the importance of the occasion caused him to lapse into Rumanian. She merely sat and goggled at him. What she would have done if I had not come to the rescue I cannot imagine. Had hysterics I should think. She always fails in an emergency. Thomas, on the other hand, took another familiar English attitude —I believe he is Welsh, as a matter of fact, but it is immaterial. He assumed that because the man was speaking a foreign language, he could not understand English, and anyhow was a person to whom the ordinary rules of intelligence did not apply. He stared at Tonescu as if he was an exhibit from the Zoo or Madame Tussaud's, and then turned back to the space by the window devoted entirely to him to give him light and, as far as possible, freedom from interruption, and remarked, apparently to his drawing block: "You don't say so, old cock. Personally I don't believe a word of it."

On the whole I do not think Tonescu realized that he was being talked about. Anyhow I came quickly forward to relieve the situation. Of course, afterwards I told Miss Wyndham and Thomas what I thought of their behaviour, rather to the annoyance of Barraclough who considers the discipline of the outer office to be his province, whereas, in fact, the artist must come under the control of the production department, and anyhow, if I cannot tell the typist how not to receive clients when I see her making a mistake, things are impossible.

But to return to Tonescu.

It was not long before I had him seated in my room and had introduced my fellow directors. At first, of course, we went over very much the same ground as I had already covered during our conversation at tea in the Allied Drug Trades Exhibition. It was rather dull for me, and I could not help thinking that my colleagues might have accepted my account of it without having it all repeated. However, that was so like both of them. They never would trust me. I got rather bored with it. I got still more bored when Barraclough persisted in asking about the site in Rumania where the manufacture was carried on.

"And your factory. That is at Bucharest?"

"But no, monsieur. There are too many people who look too much in Bucharest. It is at Galatz that we carry out our little work. There it is easier to obtain privacy."

Very foolishly Spencer went and asked where Galatz was, a matter of no importance whatever. Even if he was ignorant, it would have been better manners to have pretended to have known.

By the time that Tonescu had drawn maps of Rumania all over several pieces of paper, it had been established that Galatz was in or near—I really forget which—the Dobrudja, wherever that may be, apparently more or less the north-east of the place, and was to some extent a port, being on the Danube, I think he said, which was navigable for fair-sized vessels as far as that. What earthly importance was all this? It seemed to me to be merely a waste of time. It was not until afterwards that I found out that Spencer had actually had the impertinence to learn up something about the geography and climate of Rumania in order to test Tonescu's accuracy! A more gross piece of impertinence I have never heard of! Of course it was done entirely with the object of discrediting me.

The real joke, however, was that Spencer had spent hours in learning all about Bucharest, whereas Tonescu's factory was hundreds of miles away from there. Besides, even if the man was not able to pass a difficult examination in the geography of his own country, what on earth had that to do with it?

The discussion was brought back to reality by Barraclough, who I am bound to admit, was a little more practical than Spencer. He enquired about the output of the factory. The question seemed to startle Tonescu, until I explained that we only wanted to know so that the advertising could be commensurate with the supplies available. Even then he was very vague.

"Ah, yes. We can produce much, very much."

"Yes, but how much?" Barraclough persisted.

"As much as is wanted. Yes, a great deal."

"But could you not be a little more explicit? I mean how many pounds or hundredweight—if you do measure it that way and not by volume instead of weight."

Apparently Tonescu was not quite fully conversant with English weights and measures.

"Many hundreds of weights," was his answer.

"That is still rather vague, you know."

Driven by Barraclough into a corner, the little man had to produce a figure.

"I think about ten thousand levitzi a day."

"Levitzi?" Spencer queried.

"It is our Rumanian measure."

Thereafter ensued a perfectly appalling discussion as to how many levitzi, if I have the word right, went to a ton. It was rather a futile discussion as, apart from the fact that we arrived at no conclusion, it was pretty clear that Tonescu had been forced to guess. That was where Barraclough's cross-examining methods always failed. They forced an answer, but they did not necessarily get a correct answer, or even one which you felt was likely to be right. Nor even, in fairness, could anyone answering in such circumstances, be fairly held to have committed himself.

However, ultimately Barraclough left the point, very little wiser than before. So far Spencer and he had occupied one hour and a half and had achieved absolutely nothing. I felt it was time for me to intervene.

"Now, M. Tonescu, let us consider the product itself," I began. "I think that you may leave its uses safely to us, but I am not quite sure of how you apply it."

"How you apply?" For once he seemed in difficulty. "Its application. Would not that be the same as its use?"

"No, I mean—how shall I put it. How you put it on to the glass."

"Ah, that is one of its great beauties. It is so simple, so easy, so quick. You take the crystals, the specially prepared crystals, dissolve them in water as directed. Then you take one of our own cloths" (he pronounced it clothes which, for a moment, gave me rather an erroneous idea of what he meant) "and you just rub it on, so." He jumped up suddenly and quite unnecessarily demonstrated the act of rubbing the window. It was rather interesting to see the slight embarrassment which was visible in the faces of his British listeners at any act so violently and unnecessarily demonstrative.

"And then, *voilà*, it is done." Tonescu sat down suddenly and crossed his legs, displaying a bright purple sock which clashed violently with the magenta of his tie. I sat quiet, hoping (vainly, of course) that my colleagues would observe how, in a couple of minutes, I had extracted the first valuable piece of information of the interview. I was delighted to find that the process was so easy. I had been afraid that we should have to make special arrangements for the glass to be impregnated.

Spencer of course must look dubious.

"If that is so," he remarked, "we shall be able to test it easily on your windscreen, Barraclough. But are you sure there are no disadvantages, no drawbacks? To use a common phrase of ours, no fly in the ointment anywhere?"

"I am sure you will not mind it being tested," I put in, thinking that I saw a slight look of annoyance on Tonescu's face. As a matter of fact we had discussed this point before, and Spencer had been all for taking the line of assuming that of course the invention must be tested. Finally we had, I am certain, agreed that my suggestion should be adopted, namely that I should ask him tactfully for leave to test it. I know I had not given my consent to any other course, but I am not so sure that Spencer had finally agreed with me. At any rate it was typical of him that in practice he had calmly followed his own plan.

Fortunately, however—I expect it was the result of my intervention—Tonescu did not take offence. He seemed to be more concerned with the second half of Spencer's question. Possibly he was a little puzzled by the phrase about the fly in the ointment. It had been foolish to use slang, and not quite fair to him as a foreigner. Still, he seemed to follow.

"There is one little difficulty," he admitted rather grudgingly.

"Ah!" My colleagues were ready to swoop down on the whole thing and banish for ever my introduction.

"It is," went on Tonescu, "highly poisonous."

"In what way?" I asked. "If you get it on your hands do you mean? Or does it give off a gas after you have put it on?"

"No, no," he reassured me quickly, "nothing as difficult as that. It is only poisonous if you eat it."

"Is that all!" I turned triumphantly to my fellow directors. There was no cause for doubt here. "Why, who on earth would want to eat it?"

Rather grudgingly, it seemed to me—at any rate, with an odd hesitation—they both agreed that no one would. It was curious to see with what reluctance they both gave up what they had hoped would prove an insurmountable objection.

We returned therefore to the question of testing it. Apparently the preparation took some days to set.

"In that case," I said, anxious for immediate action, "had we better not put some on your car straight away, Barraclough?"

Quite ridiculously Barraclough started raising objections.

"Oh, yes. My car is to be used to experiment upon. It always is my possessions which are used for such things. Why not somebody else's for a change?"

"But we neither of us have cars."

"I know, and I suppose in this case, if it is necessary to test it on a car, it will have to be mine, but why not get a piece of glass and test it on that?"

"Because it would not be the same thing. Unless we took out your windscreen and substituted this piece of glass which you suggest. All of which seems to me a most unnecessary—trouble." I could not say 'expense' in the presence of Tonescu, but I am pretty sure Barraclough knew what I meant. After all, he would have been the first, if the circumstances had been reversed, to deprecate spending a penny.

"Very well, but the company must give me an indemnity against any damage that my car may suffer."

Rather contemptuously I consented to this proposition.

"Besides, really," I went on, "I am sure that M. Tonescu will assure you that there is absolutely no chance of any damage to your not very new car. In fact, I think that it is rather unnecessary of you to have suggested that there might be."

I was amused to see Barraclough blush. Perhaps it had been rather a severe snub and, warned by the grin on Spencer's face, I was about to mitigate it, when Tonescu cut in almost angrily:

"I do not see why my invention—my great invention—should be so much doubted. I come to give you the chance in working with me on one of the tremendous discoveries of the age, and I find you full of suspicion, full of doubt. Oh, yes, gentlemen, I have seen. You wonder if it is in Rumania, how much it is that we can produce; you ask 'and what fly has this ointment?'; 'what drawback has it?'; 'what disadvantage is there?'; 'what danger to the car?'. You do not say 'How great, how marvelous!'. You will forgive me but, if we work together, there must be more confidence."

Quite a definite pause followed the stamp of the foot with which he ended his sentence, and then we all started talking at once.

"Always best to make sure. No offence intended," was all Barraclough could say.

I was a little slower to start, I had barely said: "But M. Tonescu, we have the greatest respect and interest," before Spencer shouted me down with that loud voice and manner which I had grown to dislike so much. His method, too, was crude. He merely followed up his previous line of assuming that there would be a test, and proceeded to make arrangements as to how it was to be conducted. Strangely enough it seemed to satisfy Tonescu. Finally it was agreed that some of the crystals were to be given to Barraclough who was to apply them to his car. Forty-eight hours later —or on the first wet day after the compound had been on for that time—we were all to go in it and observe the results. Spencer, too, was going to take some of the crystals and test them on a mirror in his bathroom.

"And you, M. Latimer, will you not try them too?" Tonescu asked.

I thought it was a good moment for a gesture.

"I am perfectly satisfied about it. I want no further demonstration——"

"My dear Nicholas, we have had no demonstration as yet," Spencer interrupted, trying to spoil the effect.

"—than M. Tonescu's own confidence. Besides, I am rather afraid of having poisonous things about."

At that Tonescu was up in the air again.

"You see? Did I not say that the danger of the poison was a serious point to overcome? Ah, gentlemen, think carefully about that poison, I beg of you!"

"It's quite all right, I assure you," Spencer put in breezily. "Most people are not so easily alarmed as our friend Latimer. It takes more than that to frighten most people."

The unfounded impertinence of the man. How dared he imply that I was a coward?

CHAPTER NINE

It is a fortunate thing for NeO-aD that I am so patient. I fancy that any unbiased person, reading the account I have just given, would see that I had much to put up with, and that only my quiet perseverance led to a successful result—perhaps I should say a successful start—to our venture.

Yet—amazing though it may seem—Spencer actually had the audacity to remark that it would be as well if I were excluded from subsequent interviews! The only ground that I could make out that he had for this incredible suggestion, was that I was too confiding on the one hand and too apt to alarm Tonescu, by making what Spencer was pleased to call a mountain out of the molehill of the difficulty of the compound being poisonous. Naturally I refused to take any notice of such an absurd argument. Really I find it hard to imagine what good even Spencer thought that it was likely to produce. He cannot have expected it to convince me, so I suppose it was really part of his general policy of irritating me.

But I was able to make use of it. That was where Spencer was such a fool. It never occurred to him that if he took a thoroughly stupid line, a more able man would be given the chance of turning his argument against himself. 'Argument' is almost too dignified a word to use of Spencer's malicious chatter. Still, as I have said, it gave me an opening.

"At any rate, I think you will now agree with me, after seeing how temperamental Tonescu is, that it will be unwise to press him any further. Your financial precautions, for instance, Barraclough, will have to be arranged very gently if at all."

"'Your' financial precautions! Aren't they the precautions for all of us?"

"In a way, yes. But it is you who are so anxious to impose them."

"As to that, we shall see how things go. But I agree they will have to be suggested with care."

"Which is why," Spencer butted in, "I suggested that Nicholas should go away and not interfere."

He got out of the door, before I had time to reply. It infuriates me that I have not yet been able to think of an entirely satisfactory way of eliminating him. I had a talk to my bank manager yesterday, but like all bankers he was too old-fashioned to see his chances. I have noticed before that as a class they are very poor judges of character and ability. All they can think of is security.

However, so far as 'Nohaze'—or whatever we eventually decide to call Tonescu's crystals—is concerned, even the obstinacy of my colleagues has been convinced. Spencer's ingenuousness was quite amusing. He could not conceal his surprise when the thing actually did all that was claimed for it! Apparently, in the bathroom of the furnished rooms in which he carries on a very undignified existence—how Spencer, who is always throwing his old school tie in my face, can put up with such a place I cannot imagine—is a large mirror over a wash-hand basin. It was, therefore, not his mirror, but a little thing like that would not deter Paul Spencer. He just smeared over a part of it, using rather more than was necessary according to the directions Tonescu had given us, and told the owner of the mirror about it afterwards. That was so like Spencer. Barraclough would have asked for permission in writing and then covered a mathematically measured quarter with the exact quantity prescribed.

When the necessary forty-eight hours had elapsed, Spencer apparently fixed up some fearful device with a rubber tube and a geyser, so that jets of steam were propelled all over the mirror.

"It was perfectly wonderful," he told us afterwards. "You could see exactly where the stuff had been and where it had not. As a matter of fact I must have splashed it about a bit and you could see exactly where the splashes had been. As for the part where I had rubbed it on properly, it was crystal clear."

"I wonder if that would be a good name," I put in; the exact name for the product was worrying me a good deal.

"What would?"

"'Crystal clear'. You might spell it with a 'k'."

Barraclough shuddered. He was always rather a purist about spelling. In fact he was rather inconvenient at times about it.

"Supposing," he said, "we make certain about the car first. I have brought it up so as to have it available, and put it in a garage near here. It looked like rain this morning and so I risked it. Luckily it has turned out wet, because now we shan't have to pay more than one day's garaging."

He was rather annoyed because I chuckled at him for his stinginess. What did a day or so's garaging matter? Anyhow, I was perfectly sure that he would charge it up to the company.

The short walk that we took to the car very nearly solved all my difficulties.

It so happened that we had to cross one of these one-way streets—rather an unnecessary one as a matter of fact, since the traffic there is not very heavy. Actually, as we got to it, there was nothing at all coming along in the only direction allowed by law for that road. However, it has come by now to be absolutely instinctive with me to look both ways before I cross any street. It saves me the trouble of remembering which are one-way streets and which are not. I claim no credit for such an ordinary precaution. It is one which I think all normal people do, in fact, adopt.

On this occasion it was peculiarly fortunate, since it happened that down what would have been the correct side if it had not been a one-way street, came someone, presumably in complete ignorance of the fact that there was any particular traffic control there—some country cousin, I should imagine. But even so I cannot think how he failed to observe the notice boards.

Seeing him come I stepped back on to the pavement. Barraclough had stopped a yard or so back to do up his shoelace. As for Spencer, he was on my left, whereas the car was coming from the right. Now, so natural and sensible were the ordinary precautions that I was in the habit of taking, that it never occurred to me that anybody else would not be equally provident. But I am always failing to allow for the immensity of Spencer's folly. He just walked straight on.

The driver of the car was so close to me that I could see the alarm on his face. There was a great squeaking of brakes and the car skidded on the muddy road right across to the other side of the street. Then it turned right round, mounting the pavement on the other side of the road as it did so, and finally finished up by hitting a plate-glass window broadside on. It was perfectly marvellous how little damage was done, so far as I could see, to the car or the window.

Naturally, however, my first thought was of the carelessness of the driver in not having looked at the notice board. I forget exactly what I said—some remark on that subject, I know. I tried to find a constable to give the man in charge for dangerous driving but one never can find a policeman when one wants him. They only turn up when they are the last people whom one wishes to see.

Of course, too, my attitude did not meet with Spencer's approval. He was inclined even to praise the driver for promptness and for risking a bad smash to himself in the skid. But that was an absurd attitude. Even Barraclough found it so.

"Nothing more than the natural instinctive action of any driver, however incompetent. Of course he jammed on his brakes. Who wouldn't?"

It was not until after we had crossed the road and found the driver quite uninjured, and been through the most tiresome fuss and formality, I suppose so that he could prove the facts to his insurance company, that I really gave my attention to Spencer.

He was not a very pretty sight. Either the back of the car as it skidded round or else his own clumsiness in falling over after it had gone, had bruised his face. One eye was rapidly closing and would soon be black and blue. The leg of his trousers too was ripped and there was mud all over one side of him.

"Really, how clumsy!" I exclaimed. "First an incompetent driver, and then you don't look where you are going and finally you must needs fall over in the muddiest place you can find in the road. Such a very drunken-looking black eye too!"

Spencer, however, chose to be ridiculous.

"What nonsense, Nicholas! Apart from anything else—and I think you might *pretend* to have a little sympathy. If it comes to that it seems to me that the carelessness was yours. You saw the car and had plenty of time to step back, but not a note of warning did you give to me."

"I naturally thought that you had seen it too."

On that, Barraclough must needs put his oar in.

"You had plenty of time to warn Spencer. I was standing behind you and I could not understand why you did not pull him back."

"If it comes to that," Spencer turned on him, "why didn't *you* shout?"

"I ought to have done, I must fully admit, but I was so frightened that I simply could make no noise at all. All I could do was to rush forward and try and pull you back."

"And when you did get to me—which was after the car had passed me—it felt more as if you were trying to push me under."

I think that Barraclough realized that his attempt to try to involve me was only recoiling on to his own head. At any rate, with a sickly grin, he tried to turn the subject away by quoting some sarcastic poem or other, apparently a parody of the Ten Commandments brought up to date satirically.

> *Thou shalt not kill; but need'st not strive*
> *Officiously to keep alive.*

If I quote it right. I hardly noticed it at the time, but the couplet has been ringing in my head ever since. It does so exactly meet my own situation. But though I long to kill Spencer, I have not yet braced myself to the point of actually doing so, but, if I had thought of it before, had planned it, with a very little more manoeuvring I might have made that accident successful. But then, who could have foreseen it? Still, I had to admit to myself, there had been a chance and I had not availed myself of it. Fortune had brushed me with the hem of her skirt and I had not seized her firmly. I wondered if I should ever get so good an opportunity again.

Thinking of this I fell silent, and, as neither of the other two spoke, we continued our walk to the garage without any further comment of any sort. I think Barraclough was insulted by Spencer's complaint that he ought to have warned him, and his allegation that he had pushed instead of pulled him. A curious comment that, by the way. I wonder if there is any truth in it? It would be marvellous if Barraclough would do my work for me! As for Spencer, his silence was easy to understand. I expect that he was frightened.

He did, however, make one remark. We had got Barraclough's car out—and why he should require an indemnity about it, I cannot imagine. A more dilapidated, battered old bit of tin tied together with string I have never seen. I more than half expect that he is trying to saddle NeO-aD—or rather me—with buying him a new one, but I have no intention of falling in with any little scheme of that sort.

But to return to Spencer. Just as we were getting in, he gave us both a most unpleasant look with the one eye that remained undamaged and seemed to hesitate. Then he clambered in. "After all," he remarked to no one in particular, "if they are both in the car too, I expect it is safe."

A pleasant atmosphere he had created in which to start our test! We were all three shaken—for the accident had been a shock. We were all angry with each other. And here we were, embarking on a drive without any particular point to go to, to test what I knew would be satisfactory, and all the while the east wind lashed a cold rain along the streets, and each of us was angry with the other, and one of us was suspecting the other two of having tried to kill him.

CHAPTER TEN

B ut anyhow there was no doubt about the efficiency of Tonescu's invention. The effect was absolutely magical. Even through Barraclough's dirty windscreen, it was possible to see perfectly clearly without worrying about using the windscreen wiper. In fact, the only difficulty came from what seemed to be one or two flaws in the glass.

I pointed these out to Barraclough, but I think that he had probably effected one of his trumpery pieces of economy over it. At any rate he was inclined to resent any comment on it as being directed against his property. In fact he maintained that there were no flaws whatever in the glass and, when I pointed them out to him, insisted that they were entirely the creation of my own imagination. As he went on to talk about black spots in front of my face and imply that I saw them on account of the state of my liver, I had to let the matter drop, especially as Spencer, who had undergone one of his maddening changes from fury to facetiousness, was making laborious jokes on the theme of what I had drunk the night before—a matter which was no concern of his— but which I suppose were prompted by a juvenile desire to produce a *tu quoque* on my remark as to the appearance of his eye.

In the end, to quieten him, I changed places and let him sit in front beside Barraclough so that he could see for himself. He hardly seemed to realize the generosity of my action, for the car was open—in the back seat one got extremely wet. I am abnormally sensitive to cold, whereas Spencer has the constitution of an ox and is quite unable to imagine that everyone else has not. Besides he was covered with mud already.

I was glad when that drive was over. Even more glad that both of them were convinced of the efficiency of Tonescu's product. I was so cold that I got them, after some trouble, to take me back to my flat. I should have to change and sit for a while before the fire before I could do anything else. Spencer wanted us to come round and look at his mirror, which was quite unnecessary.

"If you wanted us to see it, why didn't you use something movable, instead of a fixture. Anyhow I am quite prepared to take your word for it."

Secretly I rather hoped that he would see the implied reproof. A little more trustfulness on his part would have helped considerably, but the only answer was:

"And I suppose I ought to have brought the geyser and the bathroom along to the office too."

"Why be so silly? We could always have boiled the tea-kettle. All you wanted was a little steam."

"Well, if Nicholas is going to go and sleep in front of a fire for an hour I don't see why I shouldn't too. After you've dropped him, take me to my place, will you, please? I've got to change anyhow."

Barraclough grunted surlily.

"After which *I* put the car back. *I* then go back to the office and *I* get on with the work."

"We shall both join you very soon," I put in, managing with a great effort to show no irritation. "By that time, too, I shall have begun to have thought out an advertising policy."

Instead of understanding this practical demonstration of how my brain was always at work in running NeO-aD, Barraclough merely began to point out difficulties. He did not see, he said, how that could be done without having some idea of the amount of money that Tonescu would be prepared to spend, nor did he see how I could do anything without figures in front of me nor, he ended by saying, had we as yet any proof of Tonescu's financial solidarity.

"I was not talking of the details. I leave those sort of things to you. I was referring to more important matters, to the general policy."

Barraclough gave me a nasty look. He hated being reminded that his work was relatively unimportant. What he would have said I have no idea if Spencer had not butted in sarcastically.

"Nicholas, you see, desires to contemplate the clouds with his head well surrounded in them. Like Zeus on Olympus, he will issue his divine commands later."

I suppose I must have looked puzzled; certainly I could see no sense in his remarks. I am never dictatorial, but he deliberately chose to misunderstand my expression.

"I should have said 'Jove' not 'Zeus'. Greek is too difficult for our learned friend."

"Thank you very much," I said, "but I have had quite as good a classical education as you."

"I beg of you not to start that argument again," Barraclough broke in. "For the sake of peace I shall take you both home—but I hope I shall see both of you shortly before teatime."

As a matter of fact it *was* nearly four when I returned to the office, and I will freely admit that I had had a few minutes' sleep before I came. It had not however been very restful. I suppose that was due to the constant effort of bearing with my colleagues, but I kept on dreaming the same rather terrible nightmare. In it Tonescu was engaged in making a cup of tea and pointing out that the steam had not dulled a mirror which he held before it. Then he took up a teacup and put into it a handful of his crystals and poured the tea on them, and forced me to swallow the mixture, while he shouted in my ear the words that I had myself used. "Why, who on earth would want to eat it?" and went on, "but you, Nicholas Latimer, shall drink it." I woke up quite frightened.

However, when I got back to the office I had quite decided on my plan for the advertising. Simplicity was its whole essence. We would prepare a leaflet and send it out to all our car dealers and garages, in the London area at any rate. Preferably on a more extensive scale. It would depend on how easily we could get the necessary list of suitable addresses in the provinces. We, of course, would prepare the leaflet, but we would employ one of the people who specialize in mail-order work to send it out.

For the rest we would use the *Daily Mail* and the *Daily Mail* only. By so doing we should get continuity, and I have a great respect for the *Mail's* pulling power. I should have liked to have started by taking the front page and I thought we ought to try to do so, but I well knew that it was difficult to get, and almost impossible at short notice. So I should be content with a ten-inch triple column to start with three or four times, and seven- or eight-inch double columns afterwards two or three times a week, for three months. After that we could see. With a decent-sized space of that sort I could do something useful, and the announcements would be sufficiently arresting to make it unnecessary to pay preferred position rates. Apart from the initial big one, it would only be necessary to prepare about four pieces of copy, which could probably be repeated without change. A more simple scheme I have never seen, and absolutely certain to be successful, to my mind.

Unfortunately, however, I had mentioned my intention of working on the problem to both Spencer and Barraclough, and both of them must needs produce ideas.

Spencer was all for making it a luxury product and selling it at a high price, whereas I was visualizing an appeal to every car driver, to be followed up by one to every man who shaved and every man or woman who liked looking in a glass that would not cloud over. Accordingly Spencer was all for using the luxury press. He started by talking about the *Sketch, Tatler* and *Bystander,* papers which are very good for the right thing, but which I have always regarded as expensive in proportion to their circulation. Actually, of course, they do not publish any figures, but I may say that I had a very shrewd idea what they were. Barraclough was generally inclined to put them a little lower than I did, but then he always depreciated them and tried to make them out to be impossibly expensive.

But whichever figure you took we were all agreed that it cost more to reach a thousand readers of the *Bystander* than a thousand readers of the *Mail.*

"Naturally, Nicholas, naturally," Spencer replied in his most patronizing tone. "I do know a little about advertising, and I thought you did. Need I remind you of the difference in buying power of the readers of the two papers? Then there is also the old and difficult question of number of readers per copy. Which reminds me," he went off at a tangent, "that I am forgetting *Punch.*"

I could see that that annoyed Barraclough. I believe he had some trouble before about an account. *Punch* is very business-like in its methods and most unnecessarily strict about prompt payment. Anyhow I know that he would back me up in opposition to that suggestion.

"Terribly expensive," I added. "It will cost you nearly as much as the *Mail,* and even you cannot pretend the circulation is the same. Besides, one always gets tucked away at the end because there are no 'next matter' positions."

"Don't teach your grandmother to suck eggs," was Spencer's comment. "Must I remind you of the almost definitely established fact that the advertisements in *Punch* are *read,* so that next matter positions do not matter." He seemed to think it was a clever pun.

"Personally," came in Barraclough's voice, "I think you are both being too extravagant. Spencer has not yet condescended to come down to details, but Latimer's preliminary little campaign for three months would cost the best part of five thousand."

"Well," I said, "I think five thousand would be a very proper sum to spend. I suggest that we decide that whatever scheme is used, that five thousand is the amount which should be spent."

"Wouldn't it be as well first to find out if Tonescu has five thousand available?"

"He must have. And anyhow we are going to get some results; with such a product the advertising ought almost to pay for itself."

"If it catches on."

"It's bound to."

"I was for conducting a simple experimental campaign in the motoring press as a trial first. I have here——" And Barraclough plunged into a dissertation on the various papers connected with the motor trade, their circulation, their cost, and their exact type of reader. He must have spent the whole afternoon getting it out. It was so full of circumstantial details that there really was a very serious danger that it would convince any ignorant person that it was an excellent campaign. But in all, it only added up to about seven hundred and fifty pounds—I think it was seven hundred and thirty-one pounds, twelve and six—Barraclough always went down to halfpennies—plus the cost of art work and blocks, "of which" he concluded, after whirling figures round our heads for what seemed like an hour, "I have not yet completed the estimate. It depends on what style of drawing Latimer uses, whether he wants line drawings or halftones, in which case I shall have to consider the screens of the different papers—I believe one of them insists on photogravure—and the varying breadths of their columns and pages and so on. But one could give Tonescu an approximate idea."

Spencer looked at the ceiling.

"Do we propose to approach Tonescu in a body with three different ideas, or shall we go one after the other? Or is it conceivable that two of us are going to give way? Because otherwise it seems to me that it will be a little confusing for him. I suppose the ultimate decision will have to rest with him, and as he knows nothing about the English press, I should think he would probably toss up."

"The production policy of the agency," I put in quietly, "should be laid down by the production manager—which is me."

"The choice of media," Barraclough parodied, "should be made by the director whose duty it is to know as much as is possible about the press—which is me."

"In order to sell a campaign, complete confidence in that campaign is necessary for the man whose duty it is to obtain the signature of the client—which is me." Spencer's grammar was always poor.

"Really—what nonsense you both talk." I could not resist telling them.

"Supposing," went on Spencer, "we save Tonescu the trouble of tossing by doing it ourselves?"

"Supposing"—I think Barraclough parodied him deliberately —"that we found out what he is prepared to spend."

"Supposing," my imitation was deliberate, and so done that they knew that it was, "that we made up our minds according to the dictates of reason. After all, this is a subject on which I speak with authority."

For some reason which I cannot pretend to understand, Spencer saw fit to whistle 'The Dead March in Saul', and Barraclough to smile to himself. Eventually Spencer's inharmonious performance ended.

"I think," he said, "that my ideas are in the nature of two thousand pounds. Now we must produce an agency policy of some sort, and I see very little chance of our agreeing on this—or for that matter on anything else. So I think we had better construct a little story for comrade Tonescu."

"Which is?" Barraclough seemed interested.

"That there are three alternative courses, all equally right, and the choice of them depends on the £ s. d. available."

"A sordid view," I commented.

"But sordidness is necessary. Therefore let us find out the extent to which Tonescu is prepared to stump up, and adopt that plan which is nearest in price. I think I can tell a tale to cover that idea—if I am left to myself."

"Ignoring the implication—and in fact you would do much better to let me handle him—after all I met him first—I am prepared to agree to both parts of your suggestion. After all, you must do your part sometimes, and even a man who knows little of the English press is bound to see the superiority of my simple plan."

"As to the second half of Spencer's plan, I agree. I am content to see him put forward the proposition, and I am sure that he will only succeed in getting my more modest ideas accepted. But you must promise, Spencer, not to push your own more than the others."

Seeing that he was about to get his own way, Spencer became all amiability. He was all, he said, for selling whatever he could, and he really did not mind which.

"Sell him all three if I can," he added laughingly.

CHAPTER ELEVEN

* * *

Of course it was preposterous. But it was exactly like Spencer. He would try to be funny and there was no knowing what unsuitable occasion he would not take as an opening for his alleged wit, or what quite serious event he would not regard as comic.

As a matter of fact I am almost convinced that there is no room in advertising for humour. There have, I know, been advertisements which have made us laugh, but how many of them have had any selling value? Very few, I think, despite occasional brilliant examples. Perhaps even, if the truth were known, some of those which have made us laugh most have had very little solid results. You see, advertising, to be useful, must be continuous; the message must be drummed into the minds of the public until they react automatically, and a joke, when you know it too well, begins to pall; and once you have annoyed a reader, your whole appeal is more than lost. While if the joke never amuses———!

But I am straying away to the question of actual copy. What Spencer was doing was to treat the whole subject flippantly.

Besides, there were so many fundamentally wrong conceptions in his ideas. To produce three campaigns founded on different bases was in itself absurd. To talk about tossing up as to which should be adopted was ridiculous. Such matters should be approached with the utmost seriousness.

But even worse was the idea that the client should choose. Spencer was always encouraging clients to think that they had some say in the matter, with the result that they were encouraged to talk about all kinds of things about which they knew nothing, and all clients cling to the fallacy that because they know how something is manufactured, they are therefore likely to be able to give advice about how it should be advertised. The right thing to do is for the client to state the size of his appropriation; that is to say how much money he is prepared to spend, and leave everything else to us.

Could I get Spencer to see that? Well, in a sense, yes. He was prepared to agree that it was the ideal, but it was quite impossible to induce him even to try to persuade the client to consent. He persisted in the theory that the final word must rest with the advertiser, not with us, and that even if they were wrong in some of their ideas, they had to be humoured. Otherwise, he said, they would simply leave us. Accordingly, he took everything, choice of papers, Thomas's drawings, even my copy, and submitted it to the criticism of somebody who knew nothing whatever about the science of advertising, simply because that somebody was going to pay. Of course every suggestion made to us was merely troublesome and detrimental, and the final results were worse. Then, with a complete absence of logic, both the advertisers and Spencer would complain because those results were unsatisfactory.

So far as Tonescu was concerned, we had not yet got on to the question of copy, but it was abundantly clear that the colleague, to whom I was so unfortunately yoked, was going to go on in the same way. He was going to submit all the schemes to Tonescu at once and see which he liked, simply from being too lazy to face the issue as to which was really best. My own belief is that in his heart of hearts he knew I was right and so he firmly refused to listen to my arguments because he would have no reply. However, there it was. He insisted on infringing on the duties of Barraclough's department and borrowing his rate cards, so as to work out a campaign in *Punch* and the *Bystander* and so on, to cost two thousand. He made Barraclough check it and he made Miss Wyndham type out estimates galore. The amount of stationery used was prodigious.

I believe that he secretly wanted me immediately to write copy and produce art work for all three, only that it was obviously impossible to turn out work at the rate he wanted to go, and, moreover, he knew perfectly well that I should refuse to do anything so foolish.

What, however, really shocked me, was that he went to work behind my back. Full of his self-satisfied idea that he would get on better without me, he made an appointment with Tonescu without telling me that he intended to do so, and even went off to keep it without telling me. He even tried to keep Barraclough in the dark.

Not a word did he say to either of us until he came into the office, grinning all over his silly red face and giggling inanely. He insisted on getting us both together, apparently thinking that he was about to enjoy a spectacular triumph.

"I've done it," he chortled. "I think it's the funniest thing I've ever heard of."

"Done *what?*" I asked, a little irritably. All this crowing about something unknown was tiresome.

"I have sold Tonescu this." He pushed across an estimate duly signed by Tonescu, "And this—and this---" he went on, throwing sheet after sheet on the table. "In fact, I have got him to agree to the whole of the three campaigns." He began to laugh again.

"I cannot see anything humorous," I put in, in an attempt to quieten the noise.

"What! To sell a man three separate campaigns because we could not agree which of the three was best. I think it's damned funny."

"You'll laugh the other side of your face when the campaigns fail because of their inherent contradictions."

"Why should they? There is no need to make them contradictory. Part of one of them may be wasted, perhaps, but that will be the worst which can happen. Perhaps it would be as well not to 'key' your copy too clearly, in case Tonescu should see that one paper is not pulling its full weight."

There I was prepared to agree with him. I never am very fond of 'keying'—of attaching a coupon or a request to write to a particular address, so that it can be seen what paper was the source of the enquiry or the order.

"You will have to look pretty slippy in getting the stuff ready for Tonescu to approve," Spencer went on.

"Considering the rush there will be, is that formality necessary?"

Both of us knew quite well that we were on the verge of our old argument as to the extent of the criticism permissible for a client. We might very well have started on it, although both Spencer and I were really very well aware that it was in reality futile, since my reason and Spencer's obstinacy would never budge, but, before we could do so, Barraclough cut in.

"You didn't happen to talk about finance, did you?"

Spencer wriggled a little uneasily. Considering how much Barraclough had insisted on testing Tonescu's financial soundness, he must have known that he had no right to go as far as he had without the point being satisfactorily settled—of course I was sure there would be no trouble, but still, he ought to have considered Barraclough's susceptibilities.

As it was, he tried to bluff it out.

"Oh, no. I left that for you to deal with."

"I see. It will look so well if I go and raise questions now. First you get him confidingly to sign all these estimates, obligingly leaving to us many details, including the actual dates, to a very broad extent———"

"Well, I wasn't sure when Nicholas would be ready. Nor of the dates when some of these things go to press."

"Quite. But after Tonescu has done just what we ask in every way, then you leave me to go round and tell him we are not quite sure of his financial standing or integrity. It hardly makes it easier."

"Oh, you'll get round that," was Spencer's airy comment.

"As a matter of fact," went on Barraclough drily, "I have."

"Eh?"

"Yes. I anticipated the action you were likely to take and I went round and saw Tonescu yesterday. I must admit I did not get all the financial guarantees I should have liked, but I got what I could. With careful watching I think we may take the risk."

"Of all the damned impertinence!" Spencer rapped out. "You might have queered my pitch completely."

"I had to take that risk; you apparently did not consider it."

I thought it was wise to part them by making a slight change in the conversation.

"Hadn't we better get down to the practical problems confronting us? This whole thing, since it was taken out of my hands, seems to have been approached in so irregular a manner that I hardly know where I am. All I know is that I am responsible for producing a great deal of work."

At that Spencer banged the table with his fist.

"Can't either of you say a civil word? Is this all the thanks I get for selling ten thousand pounds of advertising?"

"Considering that I introduced this account. And half the campaign you have sold is mine."

"As a matter of fact"—I disliked the way Barraclough was

always starting his sentences with 'as a matter of fact'. He was deliberately implying that he alone stuck to facts—"I practically sold him the campaign myself yesterday. I took along the carbon copies and told him what you were going to propose. We had quite a long talk and I explained the advantages of all of it, and told him you would bring the actual papers for him to sign when you came. I had to pretend I knew the time you were going to see him, but otherwise it just went off quite naturally. So you see, I am not quite sure you did all the selling, although, no doubt, you put it very well."

"By the way," he added after a short pause, "Tonescu must have fully understood my hint that it was better not to mention my visit to you. I am beginning to think that Tonescu is an even shrewder man than I thought."

Spencer for once had nothing to say. His face was such a study in mortification that I could not restrain my laughter. Of course that annoyed him and so he turned nasty, but even he could think of no really adequate retort.

"Laugh, Punchinello," was all he could think of.

"Thank you, I will. This time it really does strike me as funny. All the same, there is no need to call me names."

"Talking of names, what are we going to call this stuff?" I suppose Barraclough thought it wise to try to start a fresh topic.

"I told you," I said. "'Krystal Klear'."

"Doesn't give you the idea of cars," objected Spencer. "Why not 'Glasspo', following on the name of 'Gospo'. You start from something well known and established as a sound thing."

"And are mixed up with it for ever after. Besides, the Gospo people might object."

"I don't think it would actually contravene the regulations about Trade Names."

Barraclough would think of that sort of argument.

"I had some other ideas," I went on. "'Clerevue', for instance, or

'Nevercloud', or 'Alclear'. Perhaps 'Everclere' would be best. Or 'No-Haze'.

"Rotten," reflected Spencer, comprehensively, and unnecessarily rudely. "None of them suggest glass, to begin with. I suggest 'Clear Glass'—spelt however you like."

"Personally I should prefer 'see-clear', or something like that." This was Barraclough's suggestion and actually I thought it the worst of the lot; but at this moment Spencer thought it necessary to try to be funny. He jumped up and pretended to imitate a Punch and Judy show.

"Here we are again," he shouted; "the great knockabout comedians. Every subject reduced to the impossible triangle." And with that he started making the noise made by Punch when he beats Judy.

It was almost a minute before he saw that neither of us were amused. Even then he was not abashed.

"Well, what do you two cheerful people suggest? This time we can't adopt all three. So I suppose we shall have to toss up."

"Really," I protested.

"Tossing up for three is very complicated. We ought to keep a dice, since that's got six sides, or one of those crown and anchor things, and apportion them in pairs to us. With the crown representing Nicholas—at least in his own view—or doesn't that dice go that way?"

"We are discussing," I broke in, "the proper name for this product."

"And I was pointing out the difficulty of reaching a decision," Spencer replied, quite undeterred by the snub. "Last time we really left it to Tonescu. Supposing we ring him up?"

Before either of us could stop him he had picked up the receiver and told Miss Wyndham to get Tonescu and put him through to my room where we all were.

I hardly thought that Spencer's way of breaking the subject to Tonescu was tactful.

"We have been discussing the name of your crystals. I just wondered if you had any ideas. What? Oh, you registered that, did you? How do you spell it? Si? Oh, in Rumania. Yes, I see. No, we shouldn't be bound by that. Quite. Still, it might do."

(Hardly a good way to put it, I thought, but one could do nothing except let Spencer finish his telephone conversation.)

"Yes, I see your point. Yes, a lucky coincidence. Thank you very much. Good-bye."

He put the receiver down and turned to us.

"Curious, that," he said. "They gave it a name in Rumania after the place where it was made. Galatz-si. I gather they registered it in some way. Tonescu agrees that we are not bound to use it, but there it is."

"The Galatz rather suggests glass," I was quick enough to notice. "And it ends 'see'," added Barraclough.

"Spelt 'si'. I suppose that is some Rumanian word or termination."

As to that, neither of us had any idea at all, but at any rate, out of pure weariness of trying to think of something else, I consented to adopt it. There are objections, but it has point and there is a reason for using it, which is an advantage. But how very much better several of my suggestions would have been.

CHAPTER TWELVE

However, there was no time to spare to argue about it any further. I had done my best, and as my suggestions had not been entirely adopted, I could not be blamed if anything did go wrong. But for once I had very little fear of that. It was such a marvellous product that no amount of muddling by Spencer or Barraclough could prevent me from establishing it on the market as a triumphant success.

But it never does to take too short-sighted a view. This was going to be a triumph. People would talk about it and about its advertising. It was a great opportunity to show other advertisers how good the work of NeO-aD was.

I pointed that out to Barraclough and added that we could fairly say that we had designed the whole thing from its inception. But of course Barraclough must needs try to crab my efforts.

"Except the choice of which campaign. And its name. And its price—which involves really its sales policy. And its financing. All of which Tonescu did."

"How absurd you are. Why, Tonescu admits himself that he knows nothing of how to sell things in this country."

"Nevertheless he seems to have made up our minds for us."

I gave it up. The whole attitude was so inevitably designed to repress productive work. A little encouragement is absolutely essential to me if I am to work properly, and both my colleagues take the greatest care never to give me a kind word of any sort. It is so unnecessary. It is not as if I were a conceited man.

At any rate I saw that I must devote my whole attention to the question of copy, but no sooner had I settled down and begun to jot down a few suggestions for headlines, than I was interrupted. I had just written "And now—the ever clear windscreen" and crossed it out (I was afraid that Spencer might remember its recent use for Henriques), when Miss Wyndham came in to say that the *Practitioner* had rung up, clamouring for Flukil's copy. That fellow Flukil was a perfect curse! Of course I told Miss Wyndham that the *Practitioner* being a recent extension of Flukil's activities—it was only the second insertion—the same copy would have to be repeated unless she could find something suitable that we had used previously in the *Chemist and Druggist*.

"Oh, but really, Mr. Latimer. I couldn't possibly do that. Not really."

Silly, chattering female! I asked what it was that she couldn't do 'really'.

"I couldn't take the responsibility of deciding which to put in."

"Well, go and ask Mr. Barraclough, then."

I turned back to the question of Galatz-si. I should have trouble with Barraclough later, I knew. He would be sure to complain that the choice of Flukil's copy was not his business, but that would only give me an opportunity to point out how enormous a proportion of the work of the agency on Galatz-si had been done by me. I had found the client; I had helped to decide the plan of campaign, the name, everything except the finance and the actual typing of the estimates and getting them signed—in short I had carried them through all their problems, but when it came to my side of the work—much the longest and hardest, as well as being the portion that involved all the brains—I should get no help from either of them. I must admit that I should not ask for it, not because I should not be glad of any assistance, but simply because they were incapable of giving it.

However, there was no time to waste in considering my difficulties. Once more I began to put down headlines. "Rain, rain, go to Spain---" was the first. An idea, perhaps, but not strictly relevant. "Perfect visibility" was another line of approach. Then, with a memory of a well-known slogan about tawny port, I added —"With sunshine in our hearts and windscreen glasses". Somehow or other I was not really satisfied with any of them. They were not perfect, and I was never satisfied with less.

On the whole I decided that the copy must be more explanatory, must tell the 'reason why' story, must carry conviction more quickly. Ideas began to float in my mind; I closed my eyes to let them come more readily; in another moment I was sure that some really hundred-per-cent satisfactory thought would arrive. It was on the verge of taking shape—the perfect phrase was just about to be born—when suddenly the door opened and Spencer walked in.

"Well, really, Latimer. Considering that at last it really is your turn to do something, I do think you might keep awake."

It was no good. I motioned him out of the room with a wave of my hand, but I could not recapture my thoughts. The opportunity was gone. It was extremely unlikely to return. Not that I could get Spencer to understand what he had done—I could not even get him to believe that I had not been asleep. Nor could I discover why he had come in. He just, he said, wanted to see what I was doing. To my mind it was nothing more than downright spying on my activities.

However, there it was. It was no good trying to go on writing headlines now, so I began to think of another aspect of the problem—namely, the illustrations of the copy I should write.

Now I freely agree that generally the copy ought to come first and the artwork after, but here had I been prevented from doing my work, and there was Thomas with absolutely nothing to do, eating his rather expensive head off. Even if we did not eventually use them it would be a good thing if he started to do a few sketches. It would, at any rate, stop him drawing pictures of Miss Wyndham, his favourite occupation in his spare time. Not that Thomas was anything of a portrait painter—he always left out the rabbit-like effect of her front teeth which was her only real characteristic—but I believe he hoped one day to improve that branch of his work. Anyhow, I should have had no objection in theory to his flattering the poor girl—she probably got very little of that sort of thing—had it not been that her head was so easily turned, and that during each portrait period she started making even more mistakes than usual in her typing, and actually becoming so conceited as to be insolent.

So then, it would be an excellent plan all round for Thomas to have something to do, even if it was of no practical value. He could draw thumb-nail sketches of rain beating against a car covered with Galatz-si, the occupants of which could see out easily. For that matter he could design the lettering of the actual word to be used in all advertising. It should start with a bold round G, and all be abundantly simple and clear to carry out the effect of seeing clearly. Then he might try the effect of a steaming bathroom with two looking-glasses—one clouded and one clear. Wasn't there a suitable quotation from Hamlet in that connection? Something about "Look upon this mirror and on that?"

I went out to the outer office, partly to tell the office-boy to read up *Hamlet* during his lunch time and see if he could find the line I meant (but perhaps a Shakespearian concordance would be better and simpler. There might be other and equally good quotations) and partly to tell Thomas what I wanted to do.

To my amazement Thomas actually started to raise objections.

"But, sir, you have always told me never to draw in the air, so to speak. Never to start before you, but always to subordinate the art-work to the headline."

This was all the more annoying because it was perfectly true. On several occasions I had had to explain to Thomas that his work must be adjusted to mine, not mine to his.

"This is the exception that proves the rule," I answered, feeling at the time that it was not a perfectly satisfactory reply. "You see, we are in a great hurry, and there is no reason why you should not start. It is perfectly true that some of your work may be wasted, but I shall probably be able to fit in a great deal of it—and very likely we can find some use for the rest later on."

Still, however, Thomas very strangely hesitated. I have never really liked him very much, but before I had always found him at any rate well disciplined. He had never shown the least signs of having any tiresome artistic temperament, perhaps because he was not really much of an artist, so that it was all the more peculiar that he should be difficult over this. Looking back on it, it is strange that I did not simply give my orders and leave it at that. I did not normally allow Thomas to argue, but on this one occasion I did. It must have been some peculiar but correct instinct which caused me to do so. For if I had not, I should never have found out how treacherously Spencer was plotting behind my back to ruin the whole agency.

The discovery came about this way.

Finding that Thomas was continuing to be reluctant, I pointed out to him that he had no other work on hand.

"Now have you?" I asked.

"No, oh no." The first negative had been too slow, the second too fast. At the same time I saw his eye glancing towards a rather bulky folder which lay on the top of a filing cabinet. Something, instinct again I suppose, made me pick it up and look at the contents.

And what did I find in it? I really think that nobody could have guessed. At first I could not make out myself what it was. Judging by Thomas's blushes I thought that I had caught him out doing some work for himself during office hours, but gradually I saw the full perfidy. It was a complete campaign, so far as the art-work was concerned, for this wretched Greyfields Company—a company, mind you, which was not, and probably never would be, in existence, and which we had definitely decided to have nothing whatever to do with! Or at least I had so decided, which comes to the same thing.

But here were labels for tins, and a design for a trade-mark—a rather dreadful affair intended to symbolize the name, apparently —and elaborate coloured pictures of strawberries and plums and green peas. There was one remarkable piece, which must have taken hours to design, of a mixed salad of vegetables, carrots and beans and beetroots and tomatoes, and goodness knows what else. What it was meant to be used for, I had no idea, but the *jéjeune* efforts that were being made without my guiding hand, made me laugh out loud. Probably that was the best punishment that I could have devised for Thomas.

Finally, on the floor I saw a roll of paper which I had not noticed before and, thinking that it was quite time that I investigated everything, I picked that up too. It proved to be the prize exhibit of all. It included the name and the trade-mark, and a bunch of the most improbable looking peaches and cherries—mixed, if you please, and far too large and too perfect to be credible—and some very amateur wording about Greyfields Gorgeous Fruit. I wonder they had not put 'Grapes' to keep up the alliteration. As I unrolled it, it seemed endless.

"And for what is this monstrosity designed?" I asked.

"The sides of buses."

"Indeed. And who told you to waste your time doing this sort of rubbish?"

"Mr. Spencer."

"Oh, indeed. And since when has your art-work—if you can

call this art"—I surveyed a bloated turnip—"been under the control of Mr. Spencer?"

"Well, Mr. Spencer said 'do it in your spare time when there is nothing else to do'. He said that some of it might be wasted, but that we should probably be able to fit in most of it, and that very likely we could find---"

"There is no need to be impertinent. I am quite sure Mr. Spencer never used the same words as I did. Meanwhile, I shall take—this." I gathered up all the rubbish on which Thomas had no doubt wasted a considerable amount of time, and swept it together with a contemptuous gesture. Some of it, naturally, got a little crumpled, but it was just as well that Thomas should know that all his work was going to be scrapped. Of course, I was not going to let anything leave NeO-aD as agency work which was not supervised by me. Thomas should have known that.

"And now ..." I was about to end.

"The new campaign."

I am not quite sure whether Thomas intended to be impertinent, but he looked so innocent that I thought it more dignified to pretend that he was not parodying my favourite headline, so I contented myself by looking at him severely, and going on:

"You will get on with your proper work—that which *I* have given you to do."

I wasted very little time on Spencer. I walked straight in to his room, and piece by piece held up the shocking stuff prepared under his direction, and at each I laughed loudly and easily. They were really funny. Then with one powerful gesture I tore them all in two, except the bus streamer, and threw them at him. I should have done the same to that too, if Spencer had not snatched it from me.

With that I walked out again without saying a word. I should have liked to have destroyed them all, but to get that last one back would have meant an undignified scuffle. I have never seen anything to equal Spencer's face, not even Thomas's drawings of

beetroots and tomatoes. He was, to use a cliché, livid and speech-
less with fury. If I had not gone out I am sure that he would have
hit me; so, very wisely, I went.

Of course, it was impossible to get on with any more work
that day, and despite my desire to hurry as to the work on Galatz-
si, there was nothing for it but to go home and try to work there.
There I could think in peace.

CHAPTER THIRTEEN

Think, yes. But in peace, no.

For a while I tried to keep my thoughts away from the unpleasant subject of Spencer. I began, for instance, by looking up the quotation in *Hamlet,* but when I found that the passage referred to pictures and not to mirrors, I lost interest. It was just my luck that it should fail to fit.

Then I made another determined effort to think about Galatz-si, but it was no good. I could not keep my mind off the subject. After all, I had tried every method of which I knew to get rid of Spencer and they had all failed. I had tried the direct method of voting him off the Board; I had suggested that he should go away and continue to draw his share of the profits; I had tried to arrange the finance to buy him out—in short, every legal method had been attempted. There remained only more drastic ones. One thing only was certain, I would not tolerate him a minute longer than I could help.

But how?

When you come to think of it, the chief reason why people of Spencer's type live as long as they do, is the difficulty of getting rid of them. *It isn't easy.* In the old days, of course, there would have been a duel and I should think that Spencer would have met his match before he came of age, or else learned to behave with more forbearance. But simple solutions of that kind being obviously out of the question, it became necessary to use one's brain.

First of all the weapon. That was quite obvious—indeed I wonder that I had not thought of it more definitely before. Tonescu's crystals, naturally. They were poisonous, they had been thrust into our hands, so to speak, so that there was no difficulty in getting them or accounting for their presence. As I have said before, my best ideas often come into my mind suddenly, completely formed, after a period when I have been thinking of them unconsciously for a long while.

I suppose that really I had been making my plans to get rid of Spencer for a long while, without quite admitting to myself that I was doing so. It was, for instance, a stroke of genius to have refused ostentatiously to have in my possession any of the crystals, and then quietly to have taken a sample of them from the tin, which Barraclough had. By that means I should be able to call Barraclough as a witness, if it were necessary, and he would be bound to say that I had none. I had taken care to put on gloves when I took the sample, but even if my fingerprints were found on the tin, there had been at least one occasion when I had quite innocently handled it, namely when Tonescu first brought them to us.

Then, too, I had taken care to see that they would dissolve readily and quickly in tea, as well as water, as it was in tea that I designed to give them. That was an experiment that I had carried out at home, and certainly they dissolved readily enough, but if by any chance Spencer felt any of them when stirring his tea with his spoon, he would be almost certain to think that they were just sugar. There would be nothing there to warn him, nor was there any particular smell. As to taste, I could not say. I had with very great bravery sipped one tiny drop, and so far as I could make out there was no very strong flavour, but more than one drop even I would not risk. Well, Spencer, as I well knew, generally waited until his tea was almost cold, and then swallowed it in one rather vulgar gulp, two habits which had frequently distressed me in the past, but now would both be of the greatest use to me.

As to the method of putting it into his tea, that would be perfectly simple. Every afternoon at half-past four to the minute, punctuality being one of her few virtues, Miss Wyndham would go in to Barraclough with three cups of tea and three biscuits. Then she would come to me, and then finish with Spencer. It would be perfectly simple to ask her to get some piece of paper— indeed I frequently did use that moment to tell her to fetch something; it was so common an occurrence that Spencer had even protested about his tea cooling every afternoon in my office, which, as he drank it stone cold always, was obviously absurd, a mere pretext for a complaint simply because it was action that I had taken.

With Miss Wyndham momentarily out of the way, I had only to drop in the crystals. There would be no need to touch the cup. After that for a while things would take their normal course. I had often noticed the different ways that the three of us reacted to so simple a thing as a cup of tea. Spencer, as I have said, would leave it neglected and then swallow it in one gulp, thus deriving no benefit or pleasure. Barraclough always made a point of not stopping for a second in whatever work he was doing—a pose of course. He would sip it while adding up a column of figures or reading through the draft of a letter. I usually stopped for a few minutes so as to allow the mild stimulant to exert its fullest influence in refreshing me, but then I daresay my brains had undergone as big a strain during the day as that of their two put together. Spencer, of course, used to grudge me those few minutes' pause, but then he disapproved of everything I did.

Before a quarter to five had struck, then, provided Tonescu's crystals were adequate, all my troubles would be over. All those insults, those checks, those affronts, I had almost written 'those humiliations', only that Spencer never had enough brains to humiliate me, would be revenged. It was a very sweet thought.

But before I could put it into operation, two more points had to be fully thought out, for I must be quite prepared for the subsequent enquiry into Spencer's death. First, there must be nothing leading towards me, and secondly, there must be an alternative solution as to the way he died.

As to the first point, it could again be subdivided into two. First, as it was known that I had none of the poison, I must not be found with any of it in my possession. To that end I would destroy all I had except what seemed essential for my purpose. I would carry it up there in an envelope which I could empty out into Spencer's cup. Directly that was done I could drop the envelope out of the window. No one would think of looking in the street below, and in no time it would be swept away. I would even take the trouble to get hold of an envelope in no way connected with me. Perhaps the best thing would be to buy a cheap packet and throw away all but one.

The second point was that I should have to find an excuse to get Miss Wyndham out of the room for a moment, but that, as I have already explained, was so usual as to require no comment at all.

That point was easy. I really could see nothing to connect me at all with the event—except that we were known to quarrel. But for that matter Barraclough and he were on very nearly as bad terms. I toyed with the idea of so arranging things that the blame should rest on Barraclough, but ultimately I gave it up. For one thing, it would raise up an active enemy with personal reasons for enquiring into how Spencer died. For another, Barraclough would still be useful to me in doing the donkey work of NeO-aD.

For very much the same reason I dismissed the idea of trying to implicate Thomas or Miss Wyndham. Besides, in their cases, though I imagine that they must naturally dislike Spencer, the motive would not be strong enough. But on every ground it would be very much better if I could make it appear that it was either suicide or an accident. Well, if people chose to think it was suicide, I did not mind, but knowing Spencer as I did, I could not think of any way of making it plausible. To commit suicide you must be unhappy, be conscious of some impending calamity or of having failed ignominiously; and Spencer was an incurable optimist with a hide like a rhinoceros. It would be much more likely that someone of my delicate artistic temperament would be driven to that. But Spencer—no!

An accident then. Not a very easy thing to arrange, but not, I felt, beyond my brain.

The first point to work on was that there were actually in the drawer of Spencer's table some of the crystals with which he would be poisoned. He had put them in a small flat tin, which had once contained that filthy and useless stuff, Flukil. I had seen him produce the tin when he asked Barraclough to let him have some to experiment with on the mirror, and I had noticed a day or so ago that the same tin had returned to his drawer. I remember at the time his resenting my comment on the appropriate use of a Flukil tin for poison.

It might, then, be possible to slip in afterwards and upset the tin so that it would appear that he had accidentally knocked it over and in so doing upset some of the crystals into his cup? Not, I felt, a very convincing accident. Moreover, it had the highly undesirable effect of making me go into his room at a time when I would much rather not be present.

I might of course go down very early in the morning—an unpleasant thought—or at some time when I could be sure that Spencer was out, and take the tin away, so that later on I could throw it through the ventilator which connected our two rooms. But again this did not seem convincing. Why, because there was a powder scattered on the floor, should it have got into his cup? No, that was no good at all.

And then suddenly an idea began to dawn on me. If Spencer

had taken Flukil once, he might take it again. Supposing that I bought a second tin of it and put it in his drawer in the place occupied by the old tin, which I would put at the other end of the drawer. Surely any one would deduce that the position of the two had been interchanged—I could myself without risk give evidence of where I had seen the tin containing the Galatz-si crystals—and that Spencer had intended to take some Flukil and had accidentally taken some Galatz-si.

I began to think of the difficulties about that. First, there was the difficulty of his having actually put the Flukil into his tea. That could probably best be got over by hoping that he would swallow his tea completely in one gulp so that no traces would be left in the cup, or if that were too much to hope for, by carefully chosen remarks about the taste of Flukil, which was pretty nasty. The next difficulty was that it was improbable that any one would take hold of several crystals of Galatz-si and mistake the feel, let alone the appearance, for a tablet of Flukil.

That was a real difficulty. I should have to overcome it partly by letting slip to anyone who was investigating the matter, that Spencer was an impetuous man and often acted without thinking. After all, that was his character, and everyone else in the office would be bound to confirm it. But I wanted something more than that. Eventually I had what I think was quite a happy inspiration. I had in my possession an old tin of that unpleasant and fallacious cure for influenza, which I had been meaning to throw away, for personally I am quite sure that it is of no use at all as a remedy. I could take that old tin along to the office and I would see to it that the tablets in it were broken up, so that it would seem as if both the tin and its contents were more near to bearing some resemblance to the tin containing Tonescu's crystals.

And there, with careful exploitation of the situation afterwards, was my complete scheme.

It was only necessary to find a moment when Spencer was out so that I could change the tins and be there at tea time the next day. After that, a clear head would pull me through. I did not think that I should be putting any great strain on my abilities. I should be a match for any detective.

But, curiously enough, I did not fancy the idea of sitting in the room next door to Spencer all day. I decided to ring up the office and tell them I should not come in during the morning. Then I would arrive after the time when Spencer and Barraclough went out to lunch, change my tins, and quietly go away again.

Then I should return in time to be in my place when Miss Wyndham came in with the cups of tea.

PART II
COUNTERPLOT

CHAPTER ONE

There is a limit, you know, to the extent to which the folly of anybody can be allowed to ruin a perfectly good business, and beyond that limit Nicholas Latimer has gone without a shadow of doubt. For that matter, I am not at all sure that that small-minded little pedant, Sandy Barraclough, has not gone beyond it too.

You see there are three of us running this show, an advertising agency with the damned silly name of NeO-aD, and I suppose we came together originally because we all had different characters. That it takes all kinds to make a world is a fatuous remark, but that it needs all kinds to make an advertising agency is right enough. You have just got to know everything and keep one yard in front of everybody else; otherwise you had better pack up right away.

Perhaps I did not think long enough before I went and tied myself up to those two. So far as I can see, I usually take my best decisions straight away; when I think about it too long, I generally go and do the wrong thing. So when Latimer said, "What about it?" I just said, "Right. Get on with it." But this time, instead of having fallen on my feet, I have tumbled down the whole flight of stairs, and there don't seem to be any banisters to catch hold of.

I suppose it was foolish of me and that I ought to have seen through Nicholas Latimer straight away, but, you know, he's a plausible sort of chap until you get to know him. He is so hundred-per-cent confident that he is absolutely perfect that he doesn't have to say it. It just oozes out of him and, before you know where you are, you find you have got the same idea in your own head. Just at first he doesn't throw himself at you, he is what they call 'quietly confident'. When you get to know him, of course he becomes excessively obtrusive, and the more you find out that he has got nothing to be proud about, the more he explains to you that he is the only maggot in the cheese—which is enough to get on anyone's nerves.

Of course, even before we started this company, I knew he was a bit conceited; a blind deaf mute in Colney Hatch could see that; but I thought that a little bit of self-confidence would do no harm, in fact you need it to write copy, which was what he was supposed to be going to do. Besides I thought that he was sufficiently proud to see that he did his job properly.

That has been shock No. I. Whether he can write copy if he really tried, I have no idea. I believe, if the truth were really known, that he cannot, or at least, that he can only turn out second-class work. But I do not really know because I cannot believe that he has ever tried fully. He is so bone lazy that he just puts down the first thing that comes into his head. Now anyone can write some sort of copy but it won't do; it won't be good enough. To do it properly, you have got to do a little work to find out what it really is you are trying to advertise, and then you have got to think pretty hard and also have a flair for new ideas. Some people have it; some have not, but, by working, can produce pretty fair stuff. Nicholas has absolutely no flair, and he never does any work whatever.

Some of the stuff he will bang down is incredible. For instance, there is a friend of mine, Charles Fletcher, known him all my life, a really nice fellow, who had some stuff for curing 'flu. Not bad stuff, mind you—as good as anything else in that line. One day Fletcher will get hold of some capital and push Flukil hard and proper and then he will make his fortune; but it wants the sort of job the Aspro people have done, and poor old Charles can't afford it. No blame to him in that.

Meanwhile apart from being a friend of mine (we were at school together) so that I want to do him any good turn I can, it is wise to keep him happy and try to build it up. Of course there isn't much money for us in it at present, but there might be if Nicholas would put a little work into it. But will he? Will he? Hell!

He would keep the same rotten bit of stuff going week after week if Charles and I didn't badger him occasionally and then he merely alters it for something worse, and curses and swears at me because I have made him do it. Generally, of course, I make Charles do the badgering, but I think Nicholas sees through that. He has enough brains for that.

But get him to take an interest and do a job of work at it, we neither of us can. I don't think I ever knew a lazier man. His idea of office hours is twelve to four with two hours for lunch and three half holidays a week. Well, literally, I don't think he ever goes to the office before eleven. He has never been known to stay late in his life; you cannot tell how long he will take over lunch, and on the very slightest pretext he is out for the afternoon or not coming up in the morning.

Well, how can you run a business with a fellow like that? I mean it's absolutely impossible.

But as well as being lazy, he is so incompetent. You tell him that copy is wanted for one thing and he is forced to write something new. He just parodies the last bit he wrote or the first thing he sees in the nearest paper. Somebody put in an advertisement one day beginning—'And now—the new' something or other, I forget what—perambulator I think. Well, I will admit it caught my eye and I read it, but I still do not think it was an absolutely inspired bit of advertising, but as a result we had, 'And now—the new' everything, hats and beads for Henriques—we nearly lost the job over that—'the new cure' for Flukil, which had been in the same papers for years, so that 'new' was the last thing it was. If he had done any work, which he would not, for the Greyfields canners, it would have been 'and now—the new peach', I fully believe. 'And now—the new' anything has become a sort of office joke. So much so, that I have heard even Miss Wyndham, our typist, not a bad sort of girl, if a bit painful to look at, and Thomas, our tame artist, making jokes about it.

However, laziness and incompetence are two things about our friend Latimer that are pretty trying. By the time I had found those two out I was beginning to feel that things were a bit difficult. I never expected to make a great friend of him. He got a rotten education at some fifth-class school or other, and though I am always very careful not to refer to it (he is frightfully sensitive about it), it does mean that we have not much in common, and do not meet the same people. But all the same, I have tried my level best to be friendly and jolly with him.

I fully admit that I have a bit of a temper—short, sharp, and up in a moment, sometimes about nothing very serious, I am afraid, but it is soon over. Quite often one of Nicholas's damn silly remarks has been too much for me—I never can stand fools gladly —but I have always got over it at once and tried to laugh it off. Hasty, I may be, but I am not spiteful, and I am always ready to forgive and shake hands.

But not Nicholas. Oh dear no! I really believe that he is more annoyed by the fact that I recover and become my cheerful smiling self again after a few seconds, than by the fact that I have ever been cross. I mean I will give and take good hard knocks with anyone and all friends after, but sulking is too much trouble. Besides it upsets one's digestion.

Nicholas, on the other hand, likes sulking. It's not a nice thing to say, I know, but I really believe that that man bears malice. I remember once telling him in quite a friendly way really, especially considering that he was being very tiresome at the time, not to teach his grandmother to suck eggs, and his face! Well, I can only describe it by saying he went a nasty shade of mottled green.

Which reminds me of his appearance. You know I do think it really is up to everyone to keep fit. If you don't take any exercise you are bound to become bad-tempered, and Nicholas Latimer never walks a yard in his life if he can help it, and never thinks of playing a game. As a result, his normally bilious complexion has become thoroughly pasty and pimply, not to put too fine a point on it. I should think that his liver is perfectly dreadful which is why he wants to go to sleep every afternoon—even in the office— and he is developing a stomach grossly larger than it need be and at least three chins. Originally he was not a bad looking fellow, one of the black-haired rather oily type, which personally I do not admire, but with decent features, and he generally wears his clothes well. But now he is getting so fat that he will soon look perfectly terrible. Also he ought to grow a moustache to hide his rather weak mouth.

So that between being lazy, incompetent, unpleasant to look at, vindictive and stupid, he is rather trying to get on with. But I don't want to be too hard on the fellow; I believe I could forgive it all if only he had a sense of humour. I mean I cannot get through the day without having one or two good laughs. It does help things along so. But if you dare make a joke to Nicholas, he just looks at you as if you were slightly mad. He never sees that it is a joke unless you are careful to say 'This is a joke' rather slowly, with pauses between, and after that your best remarks are bound to fall flat.

At any rate, Nicholas never laughs at any joke I may make. Clearly he would prefer that I should not make any, but if the point happens to be against advertising, or still more, if it happens to be against him or his copy, then he regards it as being both blasphemous and sacrilegious. Of course that makes me do it all the more.

That alone would make me want to part with him. It makes life so dull to have to work in an air of such solemnity—Sandy Barraclough's just as bad when it comes to a joke. Besides if you are to be any good as an advertising agent, you must have a sense of humour. At least I think it is essential. If you can never see a joke against yourself, you are perfectly certain to make yourself ridiculous. Why, some of the best advertising stunts have been full of humour. Look at Bovril or Guinness. And who doesn't remember the Mustard Club?

So what with one thing and another, things have been working up to explosion point. To-day, however, they came to a head.

Before I describe the incident of how Nicholas tried to get me killed, I must say a few words about Barraclough. At first glance you might mistake him for one of those dry, reserved sticks who never say a word and whose thoughts you never can guess. Now, a lot of them keep quiet because they haven't got anything to say for themselves. They hope that, as a result of complete silence, lasting for several years, they will establish a reputation for wisdom, and they generally do obtain it. But that is not Sandy Barraclough. I think he is quite indifferent to what anyone thinks of him, and at times he will talk—and certainly he is ready at any time to write reams—but it is all terribly to the point at issue.

That is the first thing that strikes you. He is always so shatteringly relevant. He just sees what he wants and he goes straight for it, whether it be a person, a joke, a scruple, a fanciful idea, or ten hours' hard work, especially the latter.

Quite what the motive is, I do not know. There must be some. I mean, nobody could voluntarily lead quite such a dull life, full of repressions, as he does, without some reason. Just think of it. Never a smile, never a touch of laziness—some glorious afternoon spent idling when you ought to be working—never for a moment letting your attention wander or your conscience go to sleep. Just pounding down the narrow way, and never being aware that there is such a thing as the primrose path of dalliance. That's what I can't understand.

I don't think it's lack of brains or intelligence. Really he has got lots. Nor do I think that it is all selfishness, because, although he is selfish, he denies himself pleasure, and I must say this for him, that he never tries to upset other people's convenience so long as their plans do not seriously upset him. He generally quietly assumes that they will do what he wants, and oddly enough, people seem to do it.

Perhaps on the whole it is all his desire for money. He is a Scotsman, of course, and, like all Scotsmen, is determined to get his money's worth. Well, good luck to them. Personally I think they take so much trouble to get it, that they miss the enjoyment, but that is their business. But with Barraclough it is rather more than that. It's money first and second and last and always.

I noticed it first when we started NeO-aD. It was Barraclough who had saved up some money and, rather surprisingly, Barraclough who risked it. But I could not help noticing and admiring the way in which he kept the financial control in his own hands. Nicholas, of course, thought that if he was allowed to be in charge of production, he was the big noise in the outfit, but I strongly suspect that Barraclough really controls the show and is quite aware of it and always intended to. Not that I mind; I know quite well where I come in and where I don't. I couldn't run the finance if I tried—I was always bottom in mathematics of any form I was in—and as for writing copy, well, I never did think I could write English. All I was good at was just hustling around, and using my common sense and getting to know chaps. That's why I was prepared to tie up with someone having Barraclough's brains and also with someone having the sort of brains I hoped Latimer had, only he hadn't, if I make myself clear.

But I must say there have been times when Sandy's financial brains have been a bit too much of a good thing. One felt one had to ask his leave to take a bus, and I must admit I do hate having my fares and expenses bill queried, item by item, in the way he does. I let him do it the first time as a joke, but really I ought to have put my foot down at once, because I have known him to be positively impertinent about it. I mean, one must take taxis sometimes or stand prospective clients a drink, and I am blowed if I see why, in those circumstances, I should pay for my own. But Barraclough thought I ought, and when one day I put down a taxi accidentally which I had already included the day before, he as good as told me I was a thief. I mean Newgate and the Old Bailey and all that. Damn sauce.

However, despite his faults—and the most serious of them is that he cramps all enterprise by saying "we can't afford that" and so killing a good chance, I mean one must throw a sprat or two about occasionally—despite his faults, as I say, I don't wish Sandy any harm. I don't want to get rid of him; he does his stuff jolly well, I think. But somehow or other he seems to want to get rid of me.

Now why should anyone want to get rid of a harmless, inoffensive sort of chap like me?

But, do you know, really I believe he did. Nicholas tried, I know, but that doesn't surprise me so much. I mean, Nicholas is the sort of fellow who cherishes a grievance. But Barraclough! That does beat me absolutely.

But I must explain the incident.

Nicholas had found an almost unbelievable Rumanian bloke. The sort of man who wears purple socks with a bowler hat, thinks that Fonseca was a painter, whereas, of course, he ships port, and is perfectly capable of taking mustard with caviare—that is, if they have heard of caviare in Rumania.[1]

Now this fellow Tonescu had got an absolute wow of an invention. You'll hear all about it one day under the ghastly name of Galatz-si, so I shan't stop to talk about it now, but anyhow we wanted to see if it really worked, and were trying it out on Sandy's car.

Mind you, it had been pretty funny. The whole thing was upside down because Nicholas found the chap, whereas finding people is supposed to be my show. Not that I mind, and only Nicholas would have dug up a comic like that. But the cream of the jest was when Nicholas made Sandy try the stuff out on his car. Trying it on the dog wasn't in it, and the car had to be brought up from whatever garden suburb Sandy patronizes and it had to be garaged for a day, and if it hadn't rained, it might have been two days.

Poor old Sandy! He fairly hated the expense, but that didn't stop him charging it all up, plus the petrol he said he used, and an allowance for the wear and tear of the tyres and a bit of the licence and the insurance and heaven alone knows what. Everything, I think, except the use of the clock and that had stopped. Not that it was unfair. Oh dear no! Sandy was the soul of honour. He worked it all to eight places of decimals and divided by 365 and began fussing about leap year. I told him he had left out summer time, and he spent hours trying to find out some meaning in that remark, and when I told him there wasn't any, and it was only a joke, I thought he was going to blow up.

But as I keep on trying to say, only when one starts trying to write things down, which I don't ever do normally, one does get led on and on; I really think Sandy was in it this morning.

You see, we were walking, all three of us, to the car and I was chatting away and we came to one of these one-way streets, not that I want to say a word against one-way traffic. I think it is an excellent idea, but so far as I can see, there is absolutely not the slightest need to have one just there (there not being much traffic) and that, I suppose, was what the fellow in the car thought. At least I should think that was what it was, because he just came down it as if it wasn't a one-way street. Well, anyone might.

But that wasn't any reason why Nicholas and Sandy should behave as they did, not by a long chalk.

Nicholas was the worst, and really I should never have thought his brains were so quick. Without saying anything and apparently quite accidentally, he got just the least little bit in front of me, so that if I had been looking to my right, it would have been difficult to see, Nicholas being far from transparent. But I was not looking to my right, I was looking to my left, where the traffic ought to have been coming from. But Nicholas was, and though he must have seen the car coming, he didn't say a word, he just let it come on, and at the last moment that was safe for him, he jumped back, keeping as quiet as a mouse. I never heard him, and it wasn't until I heard the brakes squeaking that I knew there was anything up.

I know Nicholas saw because I asked the driver why he hadn't hooted and he said it was partly because he saw my friend had seen, and partly because of this rule about not blowing your horn at night. He said he had got so used to the idea that you ought not to hoot, that he had a kind of idea that it was criminal at all times.

Well, I can understand that. But you see the point about Nicholas.

As for Barraclough, I am not so sure. He had stopped, so he says, to do up a shoelace. I should think that was probably true. He couldn't have combined with Nicholas beforehand, and anyhow, neither of them could know the car was likely to come, so that it could not have been a put-up job. But that was no reason why he shouldn't have given me a yell. Instead of which he stood there and watched quite quietly without saying a word. There was a funny sort of look on his face afterwards too—kind of disappointed-like. The only excuse he could give was that fright took his breath away, which is frankly nonsense.

And then, of course, Nicholas gave the show away by abusing the driver and trying to call the police and making no end of a fuss. Why, if the fellow driving the car had not been reasonably slippy with his brakes, I must have been for it. He put them on so hard that he skidded all over the place. Of course he was in the wrong originally, but he had done his best to put it right. Nicholas's silly abuse merely showed how disappointed he was that his plan had failed.

And as for sympathy for me, was there a word? There was not. I should like to hear what Nicholas would have to say about getting a black eye like mine. He'd go to bed for a week at least. For that matter I should like to listen to Sandy on the subject of a ripped pair of trousers. He would have had a new suit out of it pretty quick. Whereas a fool like me forgot to claim off the driver even half a crown to darn them with. As a matter of fact they weren't worth darning, so that was that.

Well anyhow, there it is, and I have put it down on paper just to have a record of it in case. I shall let Nicholas and Sandy know that I have, so that if there is any funny stuff in future, there will be this evidence to go on. That ought to put a stop to any future games of that sort. But I shall be jolly careful. I didn't really like taking that drive in the car and I told them so and why. They seemed to understand all right.

* * *

HAVING PUT DOWN ONE INCIDENT, I might as well put down another. The idea seems to sort of grow on one.

It was like this. I found some people who were going to start a new canning factory. Whether it will ever come to anything, I don't know, but I believe in keeping in with everyone, and all we stand to lose is some work. Well, better to work than to sit idle. Not that I would make anyone put anything aside for these canning people, but just when there isn't anything else to do, it seemed to me a good plan to get some rough ideas together. Good practice anyhow.

So accordingly I asked the other two to help me. At least it was not really helping *me*. All I wanted them to do was their normal side of the show taken at their leisure, just in case it was wanted, for the benefit of the agency. So far as Barraclough was concerned, it was a bit more than his normal work, and I should not have been surprised if he had kicked a bit, but he didn't. In fact he went for it all out rather more than I thought was strictly necessary. I really believe that chap likes work.

But when it came to Nicholas, it was quite another pair of shoes. He raised the most awful points of etiquette about not working for clients who didn't exist and being paid for work if we did it, even if it was not used—stuff which was all true enough in theory but which has never worked in practice and never will. Moreover, Nicholas didn't really believe a word of it himself. He only trotted it out when it suited his book, and chucked it overboard when it didn't. But then that was his line about plenty of things.

However, I was not going to be stopped by a little thing like that, especially as Thomas was quite keen on it. Thomas likes drawing, or rather he likes drawing what he likes. I mean he enjoys making pretty pictures, especially if he can use colour, lots of colour, but he gets a bit bored with endless small sketches, and, above all, with lettering. Well, it is dull, I quite see, and Nicholas will make it so clear that anything Thomas produces is to be regarded as just the decoration to emphasize the beauty of Nicholas's copy. Well, naturally Thomas gets a bit fed up. Who wouldn't?

The result of it was that he was all for this canning stunt. He could let himself go, and when I told him he could do what he liked so long as he didn't tell Nicholas, he was doubly pleased. No tiresome supervision, you see. He said at once that he could find time when Mr. Latimer was out of the office, which we both knew was not difficult, Nicholas being more absent than present.

I must say I liked the stuff he produced—good bold designs and plenty of colour. It made you quite greedy to look at it. Luscious great strawberries and plums and fruit of all sorts, and the vegetables looked good and appetising. I told him I thought a good deal of what he had done.

But Nicholas, of course, put them low down in the mud class. He would. Just because he didn't design them himself. What he said to Thomas, I do not know, but he must have trodden on his artistic sensibilities pretty hard, the fellow's face was white with passion. I think it was a lucky thing for Nicholas that there wasn't a suitable weapon handy or I believe Thomas would have given him something to go on with. At least that is what Miss Wyndham told me, but fortunately the heavy ruler Thomas uses had fallen on to the floor, and you can't hit anyone with a paint brush.

Anyhow when Nicholas had finished making Thomas thoroughly huffy, he came in to me. Now, as I have said, I know I lose my temper at times, but I generally recover it pretty quickly, but this time I am going to have it out with Nicholas. Directly he comes back into the office, I am going to tell him just exactly what I think of him and I don't think he will like it, and if he tries to talk back I'll shut his mouth for him and hold him down until he has heard what I want to say. He shan't run away as he did today.

But I am leaving out what Nicholas did when he came in to me.

First of all I must say that he looked, when he came in, the nastiest thing I have ever seen. He resembled the devil himself with his black hair and sneering face and wicked, angry expression. I am not very good at describing that sort of thing, but I shall call him Old Nick in future.

Then he held up one of Thomas's designs and gave a sarcastic giggle, which is an irritating thing to do. It would have been more annoying if it had been a genuine laugh, but it was so obvious and feeble and forced a performance that I just sat quite still, said nothing and (I hope) looked as contemptuous as I felt.

Upon that, he repeated the performance, the 'hollow, mocking laughter' becoming more theatrical with each attempt. I think he saw that it was falling a little flat, so he decided that he must do something more drastic. Anyhow he did.

I was just about to tell him that I thought them pretty good as rough work, when he dramatically tried to tear some of them in two. Even as a gesture it was rather a failure because he tried to do two at once and found he was not strong enough. Consequently he only damaged one and crumpled two or three others slightly before I got to him. I have no doubt that if Nicholas was describing this incident, he would say that he had torn them in pieces and thrown them at me. Well, he certainly tried to throw one of them, but he missed me.

I should have taken hold of him then and there and shaken some sense into him, and literally made him listen to reason, if he hadn't run away, the little coward. I might, of course, have followed him, but it didn't really seem dignified, and he has got to come back to-morrow morning and then we will have it out. By George, we will—fully and properly.

* * *

I THINK Nicholas must be really frightened; because he hasn't shown up this morning. He has just rung up to say that he will not be in before lunch at any rate, which is just like his cheek when there is any quantity of work to be done about Galatz-si. However, that will be one more thing to tell him when he does condescend to appear. Tea time probably. The mean little brute won't miss a more or less free cup of tea.

So far as I am concerned, too, I must own that I can't do any work until I have had it out with him. This morning will really be practically wasted. Generally if I have not got anyone who I ought to go and see, I spend my time in looking at obscure papers. In practically all of them one sees some perfectly frightful advertisement which obviously has been drawn up by the manufacturer. You can always distinguish the amateur as against the professional touch—except that I have known Nicholas's stuff mistaken for the home-made article.

Well, then, having spotted my beginner in advertising, I used to look round to see if there was anything which could be made of the stuff, and, if possible, find out something about it and its owners. Then I would be able, if I thought it was a good thing to do, to sail right in and tell them the story—"Why not have your stuff done properly? It will cost no more. In fact, perhaps, less. We are very skillful at buying space."

Of course there were snags. One had to be rather careful not to say 'done properly' to the man who had written it, for one thing. For another, Barraclough did not like me to talk too much about getting space cheap. He had an idea that if we got it for less than had been paid before, that that was our skill and we were entitled to stick to the difference. We had had one or two rows about that. I told him straight out that it was downright dishonest, but he couldn't see it, or rather he wouldn't because of his infernal avariciousness.

However, there is no doing anything of that sort this morning; which is why I am writing this. Until I have had it out with Nicholas, I can think of nothing except what will happen this afternoon.

Suppose he comes in just before tea time.

Well, I shall hear Miss Wyndham take Barraclough in his tea, and then Nicholas's. Then Nicholas will probably ask her to fetch him something he doesn't want. He does that to annoy me. Directly I have got my cup on the table, I shall sail in to Master Nicholas. It will take me about ten minutes to say what I want, which is just about the time I like for my tea to get cool, and by going in then, I shall not only be sure to find him in, but to find him doing nothing, because he always takes advantage of the excuse of tea to do nothing for a quarter of an hour.

Then I shall start talking to him and he shall listen, and since that means force if necessary, I had better be quite sure in my own mind what I am going to say.

The headings really are already present in what I have been writing, but I think I will stress laziness and unpunctuality rather more than incompetence. It will give him the loophole for the future of proving to me that he can do good work. Yes, the line should be—"your work is at present bad, because"; and then I shall point out a few examples of how he slacks.

I suppose, though, that I must produce definite examples of where he could have done better. I should like to instance Flukil, but it is such a red rag to him and I don't want to get drawn too much into a discussion on details. Not that there is going to be any discussion; it is going to be a monologue; still, perhaps it will be as well to confine myself to Henriques and 'the new beads'.

Then I must go on to the more serious subject of his quarrelsomeness, if that is the right word. I mean the way in which he is prepared to cut off his nose to spite his face, or rather the agency's nose in order to spite my face. In other words, he must be made to realize that his idea that if he cannot persuade himself that a suggestion originated from him, he opposes it in every way he can, is a rotten idea, because no good suggestions ever do originate from him, hence the theory has rather a cramping effect on all of us.

After that I must end on the Greyfields business, and point out to him that he must not make a childish scene every time something is done without consulting him. That will be an excellent practical example of how business is stopped by him. Even he must see that, and, however much he may dislike me, he must see that our interests are the same and that NeO-aD has got to make money if we are to live.

In fact it is all so elementary that, after he has fretted and fumed for a few days, even Nicholas Latimer must see it, and though there will be the devil of a row for a time, it is the only chance that things will ultimately settle down.

But if he is to understand, he must hear it all—every word of it. I will allow no interruption, and, as I have said before, if force is necessary, force must be used. On the whole I rather hope that it will be, because then I shall take the opportunity to return him that black eye. In fact I think he is going to get that anyhow. And then I shall tell him that it was his own carelessness that gave it to him, just as he brightly said to me. I should like to cover him with mud, but it is so hard to keep it handy. I might try though to think of a substitute.

But anyhow in the end he will be so situated that he has got to listen, even if he isn't in the mood for it. And then I shall say....

* LATER I GOT SO INTRIGUED THINKING of caviare, that I looked it up. I find that Rumania is one of the places it comes from, so I take it all back about the mustard and apologise to Nicholas's boy friend Tonescu. I never knew that about caviare, and I don't mind betting most people don.t

PART III
ACHIEVEMENT

CHAPTER ONE

As has been stated twice before, there is a limit to the extent to which the folly of any man may be allowed to ruin a business.

Up to a point I agree with both my late colleagues. The only difference I would suggest is that instead of making the sentence refer to each other, they should have included themselves as well.

Since it may perhaps seem unlikely that both of them should have written accounts of events up to the same point of time and should both have started with the same sentiment, expressed in very similar words, I had better explain how those improbabilities came to occur.

The account which is written by Paul Spencer is genuine enough, and I have not altered it. It has been a sore temptation to put it into English, to delete all those "well's" and "I mean's", with which he has been so prone to start his sentences—to change phrases such as "anyone who I ought to go and see" to "anyone whom I ought to go and see", but to take such action would have been to make the chronicle mine, not Paul Spencer's.

I have therefore, though sadly, left it as an example of the literary style taught in an English public school. In Scotland we manage things better. It was perhaps rather sad that the more Spencer boasted of his education—and he was inordinately proud of it—the more he proved that it was in many ways defective. That the only memorial left to it should be a proof of that, is a piece of rather delicate irony.

But as to the account alleged to have been written by Latimer, that, I must confess, is to some slight extent a forgery. I confess it without shame, since I consider that I have succeeded in throwing myself into the attitude which he adopted, and have produced a document which would have deceived his closest friends—or perhaps I should say those who knew him best. The word 'friend' is inappropriate where Nicholas Latimer is concerned. He had but one, namely, himself.

There is, I flatter myself, but one thing which would have aroused suspicion in the minds of his acquaintances. I refer to its length. Latimer would never have found sufficient energy to have written so long a document, and had he done so, no one could have succeeded in deciphering it. But let that pass; I only mention it as a matter of mental honesty.

Hence then it comes about that Latimer's chronicle begins with nearly the same words as those used by Spencer. They are not exactly the same words. I could not imagine Latimer, with all the literary faults that his copy showed, putting in an unnecessary 'you know', or referring to NeO-aD as a 'perfectly good business'. Nor did I find it possible to write such a sentence myself.

Hence also it has happened by design, and not by chance, that the two accounts chronicle the events that happened up to approximately the same time.

Yet it is by no means entirely a forgery. Very far from it. Latimer did keep a diary and in it he put down all his grievances, lest the least of them should by chance escape his memory. All that I have done is to amplify and complete the chronicle of that period which was covered also by Spencer.

But before I begin to describe what actually happened that

afternoon and all that has happened since, there are two further points on which I feel that an explanation is necessary. The first is how Spencer's manuscript comes into my possession. The second is why I should have taken the trouble at a particularly busy period of a reasonably energetic life, to have spent so much time in rounding off the account that I received from Nicholas Latimer.

I will answer the second question first. I have wished, for reasons of my own, which will hereafter become more plain, to understand the mentality of Latimer, and consequently I have made a careful study of his psychology. I have pieced together what I knew of his mind and of how he reacted to the various events which have been described, and to them I have added the contents of his diary—by far the principal source of information —and the knowledge which came to me after the time that his story ends, but before I wrote it down; finally I have included my own deductions as to the train of thought in his mind and what his intentions were. These latter are only hypotheses, I am aware, but I believe them to be logically drawn and to be substantially accurate.

Briefly, therefore, I expanded Latimer's diary until it became the chronicle which it now is, as an essay, an exercise, in order to explore in a spirit of almost scientific investigation the recesses of his abnormally vindictive brain. Vindictiveness was a characteristic which even the unobservant Spencer noticed, but I wanted to piece together all the information that I had, so as to be sure of what had happened.

It is a little harder to say why Spencer put his thoughts down. I think it was just done in a moment of impulsiveness to relieve his feelings, to use the type of phrase that he would have adopted 'to let off steam'. I believe too, that he was genuinely frightened by the accident of the car in the one-way street. Perhaps even he was suffering from shock without knowing it. For my part, it is an incident about which I have never fully made up my mind. I am inclined to view it more in the lines that I have expressed in Latimer's account and to ascribe most of it to chance, but I may be wrong. At the time I summed up my reactions accurately in the short quotation which has already been included.

At any rate it is quite certain that Spencer told me that he had written such notes. Whether he had told Latimer, I do not know, and for that reason I have made no mention of it in Latimer's account. Certainly, so far as I can make out, Latimer did not take it into his consideration at all. I should be inclined to assume that Spencer had not told him, were it not for the fact that Spencer had more reason to tell him than me, if the view that Spencer gave of the car incident is taken into consideration. Perhaps Spencer intended to include the subject in the talk that he was preparing for Latimer—curiously enough he does not mention it in the notes he wrote last concerning his oration. Perhaps he did tell Latimer and Latimer just forgot it. He was rather good at forgetting.

But however that may be, I knew that Spencer had written something, and I knew that there had been a scene one evening over the Greyfields Canning Company. I had plenty of reason to be angry myself about that, since, as may be read even between the lines contributed by Latimer (and those I have not altered), I had done more work than anyone else by preparing estimates and investigating the financial possibilities. I thought therefore that it was advisable that I should know what was in Spencer's mind, and accordingly the next morning, reaching the office first, as generally happened, I looked round in the drawer of Spencer's table until I found the manuscript. It was at that time written as far as the words: "By George we will—fully and properly."

It seemed to me that we were in for an exciting few days, but I believed in minding my own business. Latimer and Spencer had better finish their quarrel by themselves without any interference from me. I did not even alter my opinion when I managed at lunch time to read a considerable proportion, though rather hurriedly, of Spencer's final instalment.

Accordingly that afternoon I took no notice of what was happening, although had I tried very hard, I might have heard what was being said in Latimer's room.

Punctually at half-past four Miss Wyndham brought me my tea and I continued resolutely with my work—I was, as a matter of fact, preparing some of the copy for the trade press for Galatz-si, since Latimer's tantrums were causing a dangerous delay. There was nothing unusual in that. I frequently found it necessary to fill in the gaps caused by his idleness.

Next I heard Latimer's voice speaking to Miss Wyndham. "I want," he said, "to see the schedule of dates in the *Mail* booked for Galatz-si."

"Yes, Mr. Latimer, I will bring it to you directly I have taken Mr. Spencer his tea."

"That can wait. Mr. Spencer always prefers it cold. Put it down and bring them to me at once."

"But, Mr. Latimer, Mr. Spencer gets ever so cross——"

"At once, please."

Well, there was nothing else that Miss Wyndham could do but obey. At that time, it must be remembered, I had no idea that Latimer had any ulterior motive in being left alone with Spencer's tea. It merely seemed as if here was another petty cause of irritation, a literal storm about a teacup. I expected that the next ten minutes would be stormy, and so, after Spencer's cup of tea, the third, had been eventually served, and I had heard Spencer going to Latimer's room, I deliberately refused to listen. To be strictly accurate, I simply ceased to take the necessary steps which would enable me to hear.

Only, however, the completely deaf could have failed to notice something unusual from where I was. So far as the staff were concerned, however, the case was different. I had frequently before considered that it was a fortunate thing that they were out of earshot of our conversations, which at times were not of so friendly a nature as to demand an audience. I was therefore the only auditor—and that an unwilling one—of the sounds of a scuffle and the raised voices which came from Latimer's room. So far as I could make out, Spencer was delivering his monologue and the black eye had been duly returned.

It was a piquant situation for those who suffer from an inordinate sense of curiosity, but to a busy man who was above that kind of vulgarity, it was merely distressing. I was sufficiently strong-minded to take no notice and to go on with my own work. The only point which intrigued me was whether Spencer's ingenuity had devised a substitute for mud.

The interview was not a long one. It was indeed rather shorter than I had expected. Before ten to five I heard Spencer return to his own room. Thereafter there was silence.

The minutes went past and still there was no noise. Intent though I was on the work before me, nevertheless I could not help feeling a slight restlessness, a gradual feeling of surprise at the absence of all noise. Usually I could hear Spencer moving about in his room, picking up papers and magazines and throwing them down; he was always a noisy fellow. But now there was not a sound.

Nor was there any movement by Latimer. A possible cause for this occurred to me. Spencer had no doubt hit him fairly hard in addition to forcing him to listen, but I had assumed that he would not leave him so stunned that he could not get up and go home. For if he had, Latimer would be discovered by Miss Wyndham or the office boy, and then obviously his pride would never allow him to continue to work with Spencer any longer. He would not only have been insulted, but the insult had become a matter of public knowledge, not to be concealed by any tale of an accident. I waited therefore for some sound to come. But when the clock began to approach half-past five and there was still no movement, I began to wonder if it were possible that Spencer had actually gone so far, since Latimer usually departed long before half-past five.

Really I had no wish to see either of them, and if I went to Latimer's room and found everything normal I should look foolish unless I had some reason for having come. I did not want to tell Latimer that I was writing his copy for him, so I had to think of some further excuse. Finally I decided that I could decently remind him of the necessity of the art-work for the first insertion in the *Daily Mail* being sent to the block makers within the next forty-eight hours, and I was just about to move when I heard Miss Wyndham scream.

I jumped up at once, and at that moment she burst into my room, failing to knock for the first time in her life.

"Oh, Mr. Barraclough, do come quickly. Mr. Latimer——" She stopped and seemed unable to go on.

"Well?"

"Mr. Latimer's lying in his chair and he's looking ever so funny."

With that I pushed past her and went into Latimer's room. I am no doctor, but I had very little doubt that he was dead. It was the first time I had seen his face devoid of its sulkiness. With all expression removed it was almost handsome except for the blackening of the left eye. But, apart from that, there was another circumstance which made me think that Latimer had not merely fainted. On the table and on Latimer's clothes, and on the floor below him were scattered a number of crystals which I feared (rightly as it subsequently proved) to be some of those which Tonescu had given us to use for experimental purposes.

The combination of circumstances made me almost positive that it would be useless to waste time in further examination. I went out and locked the door and went to tell Spencer. As I went to his room it struck me as strange that he should have taken no notice of Miss Wyndham's scream.

But when I opened his door I saw at once why he had not been disturbed. He had fallen forward in his chair, upsetting the teacup as he did so, I imagined, since it lay on the floor. In his case, too, I had no doubt that he was dead.

At that moment I heard Miss Wyndham approaching along the passage and, to save her a further unpleasant shock, I called out to her to keep out. Then I gave one more look round the room. There was nothing unusual in it except that Spencer's description of what had been happening lay on the table. I could see the words 'I shall say' scrawled on the top of the page, the sentence left unfinished.

I am not sure that my next action was wise. In the earlier part of his manuscript he had seen fit to give a very inaccurate and misleading description of myself and to imply that I was actuated entirely by avarice. It was possible—I did not know then that it was not so—that he had developed this theme further in what he had written that day, my reading of the instalment he had composed that day having been hurried, as I said. Even if I was not mentioned again, there was already far too much about me in the first part. Such a document in the hands of the police was capable of giving an entirely erroneous impression. I therefore thought that it would be better if the knowledge of its contents were confined to myself. So I quickly picked it up and took it into my own room.

Then feeling that if I was going to take one, I had better take both, I went back to where Latimer was. In his drawer, unknown to me as he fondly thought, was his diary. Actually I had long since possessed myself of the key of that drawer, so that though he locked it carefully every night, I had always been able to know what was in his mind. On the whole I think that it had facilitated the working of the agency.

But, be that as it may, I am by no means sure that I was right to take it. Had it been as complete as I have now made it, I should have had no doubt that it would have been wiser to have left it. But it was not and I knew that it was not. Moreover I had not read it all. There might have been some reference to the fact that Spencer had written something. There might be all sorts of foolishness.

Largely, however, I think that my action was instinctive rather than reasoned. In any case I put it in my pocket as well as Spencer's manuscript. It was not very bulky and I was glad to see that there was no danger of its being noticed.

After that I telephoned to Scotland Yard.

CHAPTER TWO

If Latimer had really been so obliging as to write fully the account that I have given and if the police had had Spencer's notes, the matter would have been a simple one for the inspector. But as it was, it was far from easy. In fact I had an unpleasant suspicion that as I was the one of the three who survived, some blundering detective might be so foolish as to consider that I might be responsible for their deaths, especially if he had Spencer's unflattering description of my character before him.

While, therefore, I congratulated myself on having removed that document, I considered that it might be necessary for me to assist in the solution of what was at that time a mystery. It was then that it occurred to me that it might be necessary for me to analyse and consider Latimer's thoughts and actions. It would depend on how intelligent the detective appeared to be, but I may now say that these were the reasons of mine (to which I referred above) which made me wish to understand Latimer's mentality.

When ultimately the representative of Scotland Yard did appear, I was more than ever sure that the course I intended to pursue was right. My assistance would be needed, for Inspector Hoopington filled me with no confidence whatever.

He is one of those moon-faced, stolid, stupid people. I am quite sure he believes in testing every step before he makes the next one, and uses those words to describe the process. He began, for instance, by examining the doors of every room and having fingerprints taken. I have no doubt that he found some excellent examples of those of every person connected with the office—my own should have been particularly clear as I had just opened both doors. Then he repeated a similar process with the windows— including those in my room.

On that I could not repress an exclamation of surprise. It was so far from the point that even the Inspector, whose conversation up to this time had been confined to the smallest possible limits, saw that an explanation was necessary.

"We have to be certain, sir, that no entry has been possible by any other means than the door and that both the windows and the doors have not been forced or tampered with in any way."

I walked to the window in my room which had just been inspected and looked down to the pavement some distance below. "It would require a very enterprising cat-burglar," I commented dryly.

"Yes, sir. Nevertheless I must ask you not to touch that window."

I could barely refrain from laughing at the preposterousness of the remark. What on earth did he think that the window of my room had to do with the deaths of Latimer or Spencer? To hide both the smile and the irritation at his stupidity, I turned away and peered out to the balcony jutting out from the floor below the one we were on. It was then that I made the first discovery which has done so much to help the police.

I was just about to speak when I heard the Inspector's voice behind me. "Are you in the habit of going to that window, sir, and are you likely to have touched it this afternoon?"

"Yes. As a matter of fact I opened it about three o'clock and looked out for a few minutes. It might interest you to know that the piece of paper lying on the balcony below was not then there."

"Piece of paper, sir?"

"Yes, on the balcony below the window of Mr. Latimer's room."

"Yes, sir. It appeared to me to lie as much under your window as his."

I looked at it again. "I think not."

"Very possibly, sir." The Inspector joined me at the window and saw it, I really believe for the first time. "I think it is an envelope, sir."

Somehow I found this vaguely irritating, partly because the Inspector's agreement was obviously merely politeness, and not conviction, and partly because he was pretending to have seen it all the time, which I was perfectly certain he had not. Actually I was almost sure of this because I had to some extent trapped him. It was obviously an envelope, and I had called it a piece of paper to see if he would correct me, and since he had not, I was almost certain that he was bluffing to hide his lack of observation, a characteristic which I dislike.

Of course at that time I had no knowledge that this envelope was of any importance. It was mere chance that had led me to mention it, but as I stood and looked down, the conviction came strongly upon me that it was in some way closely connected with what had happened. Remember my analysis of Latimer's plan had not yet been worked out. Still, with an instinctive knowledge I urged the Inspector to collect it.

"It might blow away," I pointed out.

The Inspector merely remarked that there was no wind. Apparently he was not concerned with the possible eddies of air there may be round a high building. Even so simple a thing as the beating of a pigeon's wings might disturb it, so once more I tried to induce the Inspector to act. But there was not and there never will be any chance of taking Hoopington out of the rut in which he proposes to travel.

It was in many ways the groove in which one would expect the police machinery to move. The police doctor, who immediately confirmed that both of them were dead, the finger print photographs, the photographs of both the rooms, even of my room—and finally the removal of both Latimer and Spencer for a detailed post-mortem—all this was just as I had expected it to be, even down to the collection of the crystals scattered on the floor of Latimer's room. Nor was I surprised when Hoopington insisted on locking and sealing up both the important rooms. The only thing that surprised me was the attention he paid to my own desk. In the end I asked him why.

"Because, sir, we are able to lock up the other two, but you will require your own papers and very likely will move them. Therefore, I am examining them now, so that you will not be impeded afterwards."

The idea of everything on my table being left in *status quo* was certainly absurd, but still, I did not see why it concerned him, and I said so.

"You never can tell, sir," was his only comment.

I gave up any attempt to obtain any sense from this bovine creature. "In any case, Inspector," I contented myself with observing, "the work of the agency cannot continue without some of the material in the other two rooms."

"We shall do our best to assist you, sir, in that respect. Meanwhile I must examine everything in your room first, so that you shall be entirely free."

It was useless to protest that he was wasting his time. In fact I realized by now that Inspector Hoopington was determined to waste time. Very possibly he was not busy—in fact I could imagine that Scotland Yard were not in the habit of using him for anything which required to be done quickly. In any case it was his own time that he was frittering away—I was in no hurry—and naturally there was nothing in my room which he was not at liberty to see. The only thing which I thought it was best that he should not have, namely, Spencer's illiterate scribble and Latimer's abbreviated diary, were safely in my pocket. Accordingly, I stood by patiently while he solidly and rather ponderously looked at carbon copies of accounts, a précis or two of my researches into various trade papers, rough copy for Galatz-si and others and the normal things which were always on my table or were ready to go out to Miss Wyndham for filing.

"And now, sir, as it is getting late——"

I interrupted at once. "It is only seven, Inspector. I am at your disposal for some time more if you would like. In fact I should prefer it, so that I may get on with my work to-morrow unimpeded. I should like, though, to send the staff away."

Apparently he had forgotten the staff as he immediately walked down the passage. "You can all go home now, but please understand that you are to say as little as possible. In particular you will not talk to the press."

"But if they ask us," twittered Miss Wyndham. "I'm sure there are ever so many of the press in the crowd the constable's keeping back downstairs."

"You will refer them to me." Then he turned back to me. "I should like a few words with you, sir, before I go."

"As many as you like. In fact, as I have already told you, I should prefer them to-night."

Hoopington waved this aside as calmly and majestically as he had dismissed the staff. "That will be impossible, sir," was his only comment. He did not condescend to give any reason, but I imagine he wanted to see what information would be given by the results of the examinations of his various experts. I noticed, too, that without asking my leave, he had quietly appropriated some of my rough copy about Galatz-si. Since it contained, naturally enough, a reference to the fact that the preparation was a poison, I was not surprised; but the calm way he did it rather annoyed me.

"If you would fetch your hat and coat, if you require them, we will now go."

"But the envelope on the balcony below?" It was amazing that I should have to remind him!

"That I am just about to get. In the meanwhile, good night, sir." And with that he calmly locked up my own door and took away the key! I am not sure which staggered me most, the calmness with which I was dismissed, or the effrontery with which he pretended that he had not forgotten that envelope; or the fact that, having said that he wanted a few words with me, he had confined them to saying 'good night'. Apparently he had either changed his mind or he wished to convey to the staff the impression that he was going to talk to me.

CHAPTER THREE

S itting alone quietly, after finishing my supper in my own rooms off the Holland Park Road—*not* in fact a remote suburb as Spencer would insist on referring to it—I reviewed the position carefully.

It was perfectly absurd, but I could not help seeing that with a man like Hoopington about, I must consider my position carefully, for Hoopington was exactly the type of man who would look for a motive, and, having found that, would look for nothing else. Perhaps in that though (and this was the first comforting thought), I wronged him. He would look for everything, even though he would find very little.

So far as motive was concerned, it must be quite clear to him that I had more than one very good one. There was first a matter of psychology, a science which would probably not appeal very deeply to the Inspector. But even if he could not see how greatly both my late colleagues had jarred on me, he must at least learn that they were irritating people. Miss Wyndham and Thomas would probably tell him that. Even the office boys would be bound to say that Latimer was idle and incompetent and Spencer tactless and rather foolish. Hoopington must therefore learn that their absence was no loss to the company, and therefore no loss to me.

Then there was the financial side. When the articles governing the company were drawn up, I had allowed much to pass to please both of them on points which seemed to me to be unimportant, but I had carefully controlled anything which dealt with finance. I had had no difficulty in so doing, since finance was my recognized subject, and when anything had come up Latimer had always said, "I propose that we leave that to Barraclough. It is his department, and the great principle of this company is that three separate brains will unite to make one entity."

"Don't keep a dog and bark, eh?" had been Spencer's way of putting it.

They might word it how they liked for all I cared. I had simply quietly concurred. The result was that I had retained, without their knowing it, complete control of everything that I wanted and though Spencer had been shrewd enough to suspect this, Latimer never knew it. But then the 'three separate brains' had never become "one entity", largely because I really had the only brain that there was in NeO-aD.

But however that may be (and I am anxious not to be self-opinionated), the terms under which a deceased director's share could be bought were extremely favourable to the survivor. I had not of course, got the exact figures before me, but I knew them approximately. Spencer, and more especially Latimer, was careless about money. They both considered that they were worth more than their real value, and they lived accordingly. The result was that they had overdrawn their director's fees to a considerable extent, and although I had made every effort to prevent them, I had been entirely unsuccessful, at any rate temporarily.

As a matter of fact I had just been about to take very drastic steps to reduce their drawings when Galatz-si came along. The profits on that would put them in credit again, but since they had died before any of it was earned, they would get no benefit from it. So far as I could calculate, I could buy Spencer's share by cancelling his debt to the company. It would be a matter of a few pounds only either way. As to Latimer, I was very much afraid that he would still have drawn more than he should. I sighed rather sadly and refilled my pipe. I dislike bad debts intensely and that one of my co-directors should so defraud me, was positively improper. It was the crowning act of a mischievous career that Latimer should die bankrupt.

However, there was no use grieving over it. I must make it up by more and harder work. There was a great deal to be done at once over Galatz-si and I made up my mind to do some of it that night, directly I had cleared my mind of thoughts of how to act towards Hoopington.

If there were psychological and financial motives why I should be glad to be rid of both my colleagues, what possible clue was there which could connect me with the crimes? Over this I thought for a very long while and finally I decided that there was none.

But if I was to be quite safe, I must be able to prove how both of those crimes had happened.

Of course, with Spencer's document in my pocket, I had little difficulty in guessing what had happened to Latimer. Spencer must have gone in and started his lecture; then, when Latimer tried to interrupt him, he must have held him down and returned the black eye. Then in a spasm of rage, he must have suddenly crammed Tonescu's crystals down his throat.

There seemed to be several questions to answer about that. Why had he got any of those crystals there? What was the last final thing that made his rage ungovernable? And how had he managed to keep Latimer so quiet?

Suddenly a rather wild thought came into my mind. Had Spencer fantastically contemplated using the crystals to play the part of the mud? And then, finding of course that they could not be rubbed in until they were dissolved, had he forced them into

Latimer's mouth instead? It was a preposterous theory of course, but all things were possible with Spencer.

At any rate all these were questions to which I had to find a solution. Moreover I had, for the benefit of Inspector Hoopington, to prove my answers to all of them, without the advantage of any assistance he might derive from medical examination, finger-prints and so on, but with the advantage of Spencer's chronicle and the doubtful help of Latimer's diary, which was of course not so clear as to his plans as I have made it.

Two more questions came into my mind, and I decided to tabulate them all. First, would it ever be necessary or advisable to show Spencer's chronicle to Hoopington, and, secondly, if I decided to do so, what excuse should I offer for having suppressed it? So far as the latter was concerned, I believe an honest avowal of my dislike of its description of myself and my fear that it might lead the police to a wrong theory, would be my best plan.

But if I was pretty certain that I knew that Spencer had killed Latimer, I was very far then from knowing how Spencer had died. It must always be remembered that I had still to build up Latimer's intentions. I thought about the whole problem calmly for some time, but eventually I came to the conclusion that I was trying to build up a theory without knowing any facts. I must wait until I could find out more as to the trail the Inspector was following. It was a pity, I felt, that the Inspector was so uncommunicative. Perhaps when I had more fully obtained his confidence, he would tell me more. Another good reason for keeping Spencer's notes to myself.

Meanwhile I resolutely put the whole matter aside and turned my attention to Galatz-si. There was now no one else to help or to impede me, and I must work fast. I must complete my ideas that night, so that Thomas could do what art-work was necessary the next morning during the time when I was very likely to be interrupted by Hoopington. It was rather an effort to concentrate on such a matter, and for once I was really rather tired. There is no doubt about it; murder in one's office is a sad hindrance to work.

However I comforted myself with the thought of the profits to be made out of it—the work, I should say—and resolutely pinned my attention to that and that only.

CHAPTER FOUR

Although the account of my character which it pleased Spencer to give, was very far from accurate, he did happen to be correct in one detail. I do pride myself on keeping to the point at issue and not wandering off into vague general speculations or into details which have no bearing on the question in hand.

But I only wish that a similar virtue could be instilled into Inspector Hoopington.

He has by now wasted a great deal of my time in interviews which I cannot but feel are most unduly prolonged by his irrelevance. After all, Spencer and Latimer are dead and nothing will bring them to life again, but both I and NeO-aD are still in existence and I am under the necessity of earning a living. While, therefore, I recognize that I must devote some periods to assisting Inspector Hoopington, I think that he, for his part, should realize that he should not make me spend many fruitless hours exploring points quite unconnected with the question.

I have indeed taken a great deal of trouble on his behalf. I have explored the mentality of Latimer and though much of the account that I have put into his mouth has been written and amplified after the proof of what had occurred had been demonstrated finally, the first draft which I made of that was the real means of bringing to light what was ultimately decided to be the truth. That is to say, to speak accurately, it was the means of enabling me to suggest to the Inspector what I believed had occurred in such a way that I ultimately convinced him.

But at first he had an entirely different theory.

Perhaps, since I have taken so much trouble already, I may as well put down on paper an equally full record of the remaining events. The very fact of completing the story will enable me to clear all thought of it from my mind and dismiss it as a matter finally settled and finished.

In the days that followed the deaths of both my colleagues I had several interviews with the Inspector. They were so long and so dull that, while I can still remember most of the details, I cannot be absolutely sure of the exact sequence. Indeed Hoopington had such a tiresome way of jumping from subject to subject with so amazing a lack of continuity, that an exact transcript of our conversation would not be the most easily comprehensible way of describing its general purport.

He began, however, I remember, by saying: "Mr. Spencer and Mr. Latimer were very good friends of yours?"

So general a question was a little difficult to answer and accidentally, of course, was rather an acute one. It would be idle to pretend that there had never been a rift in the lute. It was equally misleading and inadvisable to express too freely my opinions. A man such as Inspector Hoopington might so easily get a wrong impression and consequently cause me some inconvenience.

I therefore prepared to answer after a second's thought, with some care, but with a great deal of accuracy and frankness. "Yes, I think I may call them my friends. I had voluntarily entered into this very close relationship with them after having known Latimer for some years previously. I left a salaried position to come here. But I must admit———"

"One minute, sir. You had known Mr. Latimer for some time before the formation of this company, but not Mr. Spencer?"

"That is correct." (What had that got to do with it?) "But---"

"Were Mr. Latimer and Mr. Spencer previously known to each other?"

"I believe for quite a long time, but they had not previously worked together, nor really known each other very well."

"You were, however, about to qualify your statement as to your personal friendship for them?"

We thus got back to where we had been when I was interrupted. "I must admit that after we had been working together for some time, whilst my relationships continued to be on a friendly footing, I did not sometimes see eye to eye with them as to business."

"Your relationships continued friendly—and your feelings?"

"And my feelings." I remember as I made that remark wondering if it was quite true, but it was wiser to leave it at that, and no one could ever prove that they were not. I am not at any time given to displaying my sentiments and however much the Inspector might gossip with the staff, he would not find out how very poor an opinion I had had of both Latimer and Spencer. Doubtless Miss Wyndham would hazard a guess and call it a 'woman's intuition' in her usual silly way, but she would have no facts to support it, and, despite his shortcomings, Inspector Hoopington would have a short way with intuitions.

"But you did not see eye to eye in business?" The Inspector's voice broke in on my meditations. Having let my mind wander, I contented myself with repeating the phrase once more.

"In what way?" he persisted.

"Frankly, I considered that they did not work so hard as I did. I left a safe position—at least a fairly safe one—because I wished that my energies should be of profit to myself. I imagined that their views were of a similar nature. Perhaps they were, but they did not always show the same amount of energy."

The Inspector nodded quietly, and in case I had produced too strong an impression on his mind, I hastened to express their point of view. "But that is not entirely fair to them—I think I was always prepared to admit that there was much truth in their contention. Spencer used to point out that it was his job to visit clients, and when there were none to visit there was no point in his pretending to do something when there was nothing to do. As to Latimer, he was, you know, in charge of the production side, and he claimed that good work could not be done by a tired brain.

"Personally," I went on, "I am inclined to think that the 'tired brain' story is an excuse and that one does not work well until one has, as it were, worked the stiffness off. Besides one often has to go on working when one is tired, whether one likes it or no. No doubt you have to do so frequently yourself."

"Very often. So, on the whole you found your colleagues lazy?"

"Well, perhaps that is putting it too strongly. I only felt that they did not work so hard as I did—that, I expect both Thomas and Miss Wyndham will tell you. Still we had just collected a new and important account, on which as a matter of fact we are very busy at the moment."

I remember emphasizing the last words slightly, but during all the many conversations I had with him, I never once knew Inspector Hoopington take a hint.

"Yes, I quite understand," he remarked blandly, and then proved he did not by continuing to ask pointless questions—at least they seemed pointless and to my mind they actually were but, though I did not know it, the Inspector attached great importance to them.

"And how did the members of your staff view the deceased? Thomas—for instance, or Miss———" he looked at his notebook —"Wyndham?"

"How should I know, Inspector? I was not in the habit of discussing my fellow directors with the typist."

It was rather a more severe snub than I had intended to

produce, but somehow I must keep this man to the point. In any case it was wasted.

"Am I not right in saying that Mr. Latimer was occasionally rather rude to both of them?"

"Rude? No. No. I should hardly say that. He used to order them about rather autocratically."

"And had not Mr. Spencer an openly expressed objection to employing married women?"

"Oh, Paul Spencer was capable of saying anything. I do remember once that he made some remark to Miss Wyndham—I believe it was intended to be facetious—about sacking her if she ever got married. He ended by saying, 'You can't keep your mind on the home, the baby and the typewriter.' I remember now Miss Wyndham asked me to ask him not to be humorous in that vein. She is just a little old-fashioned, and rather easily shocked."

"I am not surprised," the Inspector commented, writing hard all the while. "So Mr. Spencer had threatened to dismiss Miss Wyndham if she was married."

"Yes, but I am not sure that he meant it seriously."

"But do you think that she thought that he did?"

"Of that I really have no idea."

Once more the snub was wasted. Inspector Hoopington continued imperviously. "And what were Mr. Latimer's views on the subject?"

"Again I hardly know. He treated her more or less as a machine, and found fault frequently with her work, but I attach very little importance to that. Latimer was of rather a censorious nature. I think he would have fallen into line if Spencer had strongly insisted; but really the incident was a trivial one and I do not imagine that any of us took Spencer's remark seriously. Latimer's chief complaint was that Thomas would make sketches of Miss Wyndham when he had nothing else to do. It is Thomas's ambition to develop his art into other forms, but Latimer used to say that he wanted him to concentrate on what was strictly useful to the agency, namely, lettering mainly and simple sketches. 'If we want portraiture,' he used to say, 'or a chocolate box picture, we shall employ an outside artist and a different model'."

The Inspector seemed unexpectedly interested. "Didn't Thomas rather resent that?"

"He did. It took me a long while to calm him down after that remark. He wanted me to tell Latimer not to be rude to Miss Wyndham. But, with the greatest respect, Inspector, am I not wandering from the point?"

Even that failed to influence him—perhaps I had overacted in suggesting that it was I who was being irrelevant. "Not at all, sir. You interest me very much. Besides sir, if you will pardon my saying so, I must judge what concerns me and what does not."

I remember looking ruefully at the piles of work on my table. Thanks to my industry the night before, Thomas was hard at work on the campaign for Tonescu, but there were others— Henriques for instance—and there were accounts to be examined, letters to answer and all the normal routine business.

But my glance was wasted; Inspector Hoopington continued to ask his questions. Now they were directed to what Thomas thought of Miss Wyndham, now to what Spencer thought of Thomas, occasionally to my views upon any or all of them. It was a dreadful examination because it pursued no ordered path, but zig-zagged wildly. So far as I could make out, Hoopington had no settled plan, no real guiding idea in his mind. He was just asking questions to learn the general gossip of the office and hoping that something would arise from it. On the whole it appeared as if nothing was emerging and all the while the minutes, which should have been devoted to profitable work, were passing. I got to hate the Inspector's notebook and the dilatoriness it produced. I even contemplated making notes of all he said to see if so prac- tical a demonstration would show him how tiresome his action was, but I was afraid as a piece of sarcasm it would be wasted.

The extraordinary thing was that in spite of his verbosity, he did not touch on the one thing of importance. Including Miss Wyndham and Thomas, there were five people in whom he was interested and he talked about the opinion of each of us for the other with one exception. He had not asked what Spencer and Latimer thought of each other—and that was the only one which mattered.

Eventually I had to bring it to his notice and by a somewhat direct remark at that.

But it was quite difficult to get him interested at all. "One thing at a time, if you please, Mr. Barraclough," was his somewhat startling remark, considering that he had been talking about several things at once most of the morning, "we will come to the question of that later. I should prefer to finish the subject we have been discussing first."

"And which of the subjects we have been discussing do you wish to finish?" I must admit I was a little rattled, although I was glad to hear that the word 'finish' was included in the Inspector's vocabulary.

But the Inspector was quite imperturbable. We went back to the question of marriage—a very uninteresting subject.

CHAPTER FIVE

In the main, so far as I remember, that was an account of our first interview, and at the time I had no idea what the Inspector's object was nor how far he was away from what I considered the truth.

Before I go into that and all the unpleasantness to which it led, perhaps it will be best to deal with the Inspector's second line of approach.

If it was not the most important one, it had at any rate a definite connection with the matter in hand, and for that reason I was quite glad when he came to it. It concerned the question as to who had access to our stock of Galatz-si, and why there were two tins in Spencer's drawer, one of which contained the crystals Tonescu had let us have and the other Flukil.

I had to explain that originally I had had in my possession most of what Tonescu had handed over to us although I had used nearly all that I had had in experimenting on the windscreen of my car. The rest was still in my drawer.

"So I had observed," Hoopington interjected.

"Well, naturally, Inspector, if you will excuse my saying so. I suppose there is no doubt that both of them died as a result of swallowing Galatz-si, so I imagined that you would look at every source there was from which it could come."

Rather annoyingly the Inspector did not answer most of this. I really wanted to be assured, although I was morally certain that it was the cause of death. In the case of Spencer there was just room for doubt. But instead of telling me by agreeing, he just went on. "And who had access to your drawer?"

"Actually I suppose anyone who could get into the room."

"It was not locked?"

"No." I refrained from pointing out that the Inspector must have been aware of that from his own personal knowledge.

"So anyone who cared could have got hold of it? Don't you think", he went on when I nodded assent, "that that was a trifle careless?"

"Really, Inspector, I had no idea that anyone wanted to poison either of them. Besides mine was not the only possible source of supply."

But Hoopington never followed up a point logically so as to be finished with it. Instead he asked if I had considered the question of whether the amount left in my possession was diminished. To that I could not give him a definite answer. I thought that some had gone—in fact I was morally certain that it had, but I could not swear that the quantity had diminished.

Again the Inspector went off at a tangent. "Why are you morally certain?" he asked.

"Because the only other person who had any was Spencer and he had used nearly all his on the mirror. If you had known Spencer, Inspector, you would readily believe that he used more than was necessary—he was always extravagant—and he left only a little after splashing it over the surface of the glass. In fact he told me himself that he would want some more if any further test was to be made. Whereas I used on my windscreen only so much as M. Tonescu said was necessary. It was more economical and it was a more accurate test of the properties of the invention. Now, when I found Latimer lying here dead, I saw myself and of course you saw too, a considerable number of crystals scattered on the floor and on the table. It appeared to me that more was spilt than had been left in the tin that Spencer had. Therefore I am morally certain that some must have been taken from my stock."

"I see. So your tin has probably been tampered with, and its existence was known to, and was accessible to all the members of the staff?"

"Yes. Accessible also, please remember, to Spencer and Latimer themselves." It was tiresome to be forced to suggest so frequently what had obviously happened, but I was really not sure that the Inspector had seen the possibility which I envisaged. But Hoopington seemed barely interested.

"Now to turn to the question of the contents of Mr. Spencer's drawer," he went on as if I had said nothing. "There was generally a tin of this substance Flukil there?"

"Yes."

"And that fact was known to all the staff?"

"I think so. Also Mr. Latimer."

"Also to Mr. Latimer and yourself, sir," the Inspector added unnecessarily. Of course I knew all about it. If I had not, how could I have given any information as to what other people knew?

"There was usually only one tin? And that was on the left hand side of the drawer?"

I nodded assent.

"Consider the question for a minute, sir. Did it resemble Galatz-si?"

"No. Both were whitish, but while Flukil was in rectangular tablets, the other substance consisted of crystals. But surely you have seen them both yourself?"

"I have," was his irritating reply, "but I wished to confirm the point. It was never Mr. Spencer's habit to break up the tablets of Flukil?"

"No. Why should he?"

"Precisely, sir. Yet the tablets in the tin in his drawer were broken up."

It was the first fact that he had told me which was new to me, and I was anxious to show how willing I was to co-operate by making any helpful comment I could. "Then I suppose, Inspector, that you think that after Spencer had crushed the crystals down Latimer's throat, he went back, and, feeling ill, had meant to take some Flukil—it did relieve headaches—but accidentally picked up the tin of Galatz-si."

"Which had been changed over to the other side of the drawer?"

It was then that I began to see that there was something in the Inspector's mind, and that he was not just hoping that information would turn up.

"So you think that the tins were changed round deliberately so that he should make such a mistake?"

"Possibly. But would you, immediately after you had killed someone, take a headache cure? And if you did, would you put it in your tea?"

This at the time was also news to me, and I had to think again. Remember that so far I had not seen quite so clearly what Latimer's plans had been, but as the Inspector's questions were merely rhetorical, it seemed best to answer them by asking him something.

"So you think someone put the crystals into his tea and that there is no possibility that they came there by accident?"

"It is quite certain that they did not come from the tin in his drawer, because he had not touched that tin at all. Whoever altered them round carefully, ran a duster over them, because neither of them showed any fingerprints at all. It is therefore clear that the crystals which poisoned Mr. Spencer came from your stock, not his, or had been taken from his some time before. Your tin has plenty of finger marks on it, but so many that they blur each other. Therefore Mr. Spencer met his death because poison was put in his tea. Now I understand that it was known that he always left it to get cool. Therefore it could have been put in while he was talking to Mr. Latimer."

"Or before," I put in.

"Or before. In either case every member of the office staff had every opportunity to obtain the poison. Either Miss Wyndham or Thomas could put it in before they served the tea, or either of them, or for that matter, you yourself, could have put it in while it was standing cooling in his room. The only thing that is certain is that it was put in by someone."

So all this was leading up to the fact that it was not suicide! Well, well, that was a point which only Inspector Hoopington would have thought it was necessary to prove.

"Let me make some suggestions, Inspector. It would be dangerous for anyone to put it in before, because whoever did so, could not be sure that Latimer or I would not take the particular cup."

"You are sure that a cup was not handed to you?"

"No. Though I admit I always do take the nearest cup."

"Precisely." The Inspector seemed to think he had made a point.

"Then, as to putting it in after, although voices speaking in here cannot be heard in the outer office, and vice versa, the opening of any door can. Now I can assure you that I heard no one move about except Spencer, and if you want a check on my movements, I am sure that Miss Wyndham will tell you that except for hearing Spencer go to Latimer's room, she heard no movements."

"The opening and shutting of doors. Thank you, sir. That is a matter into which I shall certainly enquire."

Very solemnly the Inspector wrote my remarks down, apparently unaware that he was being not a little impertinent in thus openly preparing to substantiate what I had told him as to my own movements. I think that it was while he was doing so, that the truth flashed across my mind. At any rate I think it was then that I suggested to him the course which events had taken.

"There is one point which perhaps has not been brought to your attention. Latimer made Miss Wyndham fetch some papers. Therefore he was left alone with what would certainly be Spencer's cup of tea, being the only remaining one. There was nothing to prevent his putting in the crystals then—nothing whatever. Surely, Inspector, we have now got to the bottom of it!"

It took some while for the Inspector to understand what I meant, but eventually he managed to grasp my theory that Latimer had planned to murder Spencer and had in fact murdered him by poisoning his tea while Miss Wyndham was getting the schedule of dates for the *Daily Mail*, that Latimer had carefully avoided being ostensibly in possession of any Galatz-si, that it was Latimer who had altered the tins round in the hope of making it look as if it were suicide, an appearance which he had failed to create. But that Spencer had got his blow in first, only to fall a victim to Latimer's scheme.

Even when I had explained this fully to the Inspector, so stupid was he that he refused to accept it. He had, of course, to own that it was a possibility, since not even he could refuse to admit that it fitted all the facts perfectly.

"All the same, sir, although as a theory, it has much to commend it, it must be tested out fully before I can accept it as final. Besides, we are a very long way from proof and I have in mind other possibilities which might cover it equally well."

I must own that I found this a trifle annoying. It had not been a very difficult problem and I took very little credit for solving it, and none for thinking more rapidly than Inspector Hoopington, but still it would have been good sportsmanship on the part of the Inspector if he had freely admitted that he had been beaten and that his work was done for him.

But Hoopington proved himself to be no sportsman at all.

Because the solution had come from me, he must needs try to

find some way of evading it. I knew very well that in time he would be forced to come round to my reasoned exposition, but meanwhile he was apparently going to take a very mean revenge for his defeat. He was going to continue to waste my time and to put up some other preposterous theory.

He started by asking questions about who had a duster. For some time I failed to see what his objective was, but ultimately I discovered that he was wondering who had wiped the finger-prints off the tin in Spencer's drawer. Of course, Miss Wyndham does such dusting as is not done by the office cleaners and keeps something for the purpose, I believe, but why assume that a duster was necessary? Had not everybody got a handkerchief? The Inspector seemed quite aggrieved when I pointed this out.

Then we traversed all over again the statement that I had previously made to him about what I had heard while I was sitting in my room and Spencer was telling Latimer what he thought of him. I was on rather thin ice here really because I did not wish to say how much I knew of Spencer's intentions, but it was quite simple to make rings round the Inspector. There was no difficulty, but it was an interminable interview. He even tried to find some questions to ask about my views and intentions in the event of Miss Wyndham being found to be married.

CHAPTER SIX

Actually it was his final question on that subject which led me to find out in what direction his mind was moving.

He had ended by saying that he supposed that I shared Spencer's views on that point and would immediately dismiss her. I had wearily replied that I should consider that problem when it arose and told him that as she did her work very badly as it was, any deterioration would be more than I could stand. "Typing is very important to us, especially accuracy, and that demands concentration. Consequently if Miss Wyndham were to have her attention distracted any further, I must admit that I should have to consider very seriously whether we could afford to retain her."

On that, with abrupt alacrity, he had gone. The very pointlessness of concluding there had startled me into thinking, and, once I did, it was not long before his whole idea was revealed to me in its full ridiculousness. His 'other possibilities' seemed to consist of only one—but the Inspector was often inaccurate in his phraseology—and it was to my mind a very unlikely one.

Still it was of some value to have found out what it was. It seems hard to credit, but apparently he was considering the possibility of Thomas and Miss Wyndham having been jointly responsible—an absurd idea, because neither individually nor collectively had they the brains.

When I first saw where Hoopington's questions were leading, I thought that those whom he suspected had no motive; subsequently, however, I was to learn that they had one, though an insufficient one, and it was this which was misleading Hoopington.

If he had listened to me from the start, it would have saved a great deal of trouble for all of us, but the worst of exploring every avenue without a purpose is that it leads to waste of time and the following up of entirely irrelevant lines of thought.

It appears that on the very evening when my fellow directors had died, Hoopington had not been content to stop his investigations when he left the office soon after dismissing me with so little courtesy. He had thought it right to have a further interview with both Thomas and Miss Wyndham. It must have been an afterthought as it was his proposal that they should go home. Alternatively, perhaps he wanted first to get some food himself or to think over such facts as he knew already. Why he should not have waited until the next morning I do not know, but at any rate he went off to the address which he had already noted down as that of Miss Wyndham. It is just possible—but I am only guessing —that she had hesitated slightly when she gave it to him and that that was the reason why he decided to go there. At any rate it was not the address where she was living.

Of course I was not a spectator of the scene and it was only later on that I got a very brief account of what happened, but I gather that what occurred was something like this:

The door was opened by a middle-aged woman who replied to his request to see Miss Wyndham. "You must be something to do with the office where she works."

"Why, yes, but how do you know that?"

"Because no one else coming here would call my daughter Miss Wyndham."

I can imagine the Inspector's heavy tact and his apologies for the error. He would have ended by asking what her right name was. The reply must have startled him—"Mrs. Thomas."

"Of 41 Bouverie Road?" looking at his notebook.

"Naturally. She is living with her husband." (Rather tartly this.)

More apologies would have certainly followed, ending with an innocent remark that the caller was unaware that she was married since she used her maiden name. Rather overdoing an air of innocence, he ended: "Many ladies prefer to use their maiden names, I know, but I never quite know why."

But Miss Wyndham's mother, a guileless person, fell into the trap and threw out the remark which was to lead Inspector Hoopington so grievously astray. "It was all", she said, "on account of that Spencer and the fresh remarks he made about married girls working."

Upon that, a little judicious questioning easily induced the gossiping Mrs. Wyndham to give a highly dramatic version of Spencer's foolish joke about the difficulty of concentrating on the baby and the typewriter. The remark, never very tactful, had apparently hurt Miss Wyndham considerably. She had retailed it, with additions, to her mother, who had added her own touches until Spencer was made out to have been in the habit of saying that he would certainly not continue to employ anyone who was even engaged and to have added a series of remarks about babies which were highly indelicate.

"I wouldn't have let her stay—naturally I wouldn't, she being a most respectable young lady—if Percy, that's Mr. Thomas, hadn't been there to look after her. And it does make a difference her being married, though that Spencer didn't know that. And so, as Percy said, they wanted the money to pay the instalments on the furniture and there it was, and he thought it was best that she should stay whatever either of them might say."

"Either of them?"

"Yes. There are three really. But Barraclough, he doesn't

matter." (I need hardly say that I have inferred this comment rather than had it directly stated to me.) "But Latimer, he must be the rudest man there ever was. Well, only think the other day Percy was slack, he often is up at the office, and he was drawing a portrait of Maud—Mrs. Thomas I should say—oh, it was ever so lovely, he showed it to us afterwards. Percy's going in for portraits one day, and it was the very image of her, and what must Latimer needs say but, 'If we want pretty pictures for the outside of a chocolate box, we will go outside where we can find somebody that can draw them and get a model that looks pretty instead of Miss Wyndham!' Well, what I mean to say is, poor Maud may be no great beauty—her front teeth do stick out just a little bit, though a nicer girl there never was—but why go and say things like that—made the poor girl cry it did."

Now really Inspector Hoopington should have known better. In the first place he should not have taken advantage of the fact that the murders, having taken place at night, were not in the evening paper; secondly, I think he ought to have said who he was, though it was true that he had hardly had a chance to get a word in; and thirdly he ought to have known that the idle tattle of such a person as Mrs. Wyndham should not be taken as serious evidence, unless it were corroborated by some more reliable witness.

But I regret to say that he took a course exactly opposite to this. He encouraged her to go on talking and as she went on, finding a sympathetic listener, whereas most people, I imagine, flee when Mrs. Wyndham starts talking, indeed this may be the reason why Miss Wyndham married Thomas—I can think of no other—but my style is beginning to resemble that of the good lady, and I must leave the sentence hopelessly entangled and without a verb. Finding, as I say, a sympathetic listener, she allowed the story to grow. By the end of ten minutes Spencer was an immoral man prepared to dismiss from his employment any woman who had any matrimonial entanglement, for the most sinister reasons; dear Maud was a paragon of virtue, constantly resisting the most dazzling temptations that he hung before her; and Latimer was a brutal bully whom she loathed almost as much as she despised and detested, the profligate Spencer.

Really Inspector Hoopington should have recognized the phrases of the penny novelette; perhaps in a minute or two more he would have done so, if at that moment Miss Wyndham had not arrived and exclaimed: "Why, good gracious me, mother, whatever are you saying to the Inspector?"

It was then that Mrs. Wyndham apparently excelled herself to Miss Wyndham's lasting confusion. Indeed, she ascribes Hoopington's subsequent attempt to fasten the crime on to her to be merely a petty desire to revenge himself for it. But low though my opinion of that officer is, I do not think so poorly of him as that.

Anyhow, Mrs. Wyndham apparently exclaimed: "The Inspector? The *Police?* Why, I thought I was talking to a gentleman!"

"Oh, but, Mother, Inspector Hoopington is a gentleman, although he is in Scotland Yard."

It was a good attempt at a recovery, but Mrs. Wyndham was quite unable to see any necessity for it. Indeed when she found out that he had induced her to talk freely about two people who were murdered, her attitude to the Inspector fell to below freezing point. It was one of her cardinal principles that she should never in any circumstances say anything derogatory of the dead, and the fact that Spencer and Latimer had met a violent and sudden end made it, to her mind, all the more essential to be laudatory. Personally I can never see any sense in the attitude—indeed I have been very fully and impartially considering the characters of both my late colleagues—but, given her premises, Inspector Hoopington had certainly put her in a false position. Perhaps she suffered, too, from a twinge of conscience on account of the exaggerations in which she had permitted herself to indulge.

Apparently she objected so much that she tried to prevent him from questioning her daughter at all. But here the Inspector was too skilful. He induced Miss Wyndham, or rather Mrs. Thomas, to return to her husband and interviewed them both in their own house, free from the torrent of the parental eloquence. But what he found out there I do not know—nothing I should imagine.

But I am anticipating events. At the time when it first occurred to me that Hoopington was attempting to throw the blame on to the Thomases, I was unaware of all this, unaware, even that they were married—a subject on which as a matter of fact I, too, had strong views, but I never express my opinion on that class of matter until the necessity arises. But that is in the future. At the time I had merely to contemplate what I should do as a result of Hoopington's suspicions.

I was convinced that he was wrong. In fact I knew he was, since I had solved the problem entirely to my own satisfaction.

The question was whether I should attempt to stop him going on with it. Supposing that he actually accused them? It would no doubt be unpleasant for them, but that was no concern of mine. Supposing they were actually tried? Again my first thought was that it did not interest me. It was entirely their affair, and since they were innocent, they would presumably not be hanged. Even if they were, it was nothing to do with me.

But on further consideration I saw that there was a flaw in this argument.

The disturbance which would be caused would be a very considerable inconvenience. Incompetent though both of them were, or at least, to be fair, not more than passably competent though they were, they were temporarily necessary to me. I could easily replace them in time, if it was imperative or desirable, but I did not wish to do so until the Galatz-si campaign was entirely ready to be launched. That was only a question of days, but until it was, I wished to play for time. The removal of Latimer and Spencer had made things easier rather than harder. The removal of Thomas would be a nuisance.

Accordingly I made up my mind to devote still more of my precious hours to listening to Inspector Hoopington. I would express my strong feelings that Thomas and Miss Wyndham were not concerned, and that I hoped he would at least hold his hand and not take any active steps for a few days. I ought to be able to convince him; at any rate I must delay him, and meanwhile I had got Tonescu's personal guarantee and a bank reference from Rumania; also a deposit on the advertising. It would be safe to go ahead with that and I could get started if Thomas had even only forty-eight hours more to complete his work.

After that I should be indifferent as to what the Inspector did.

CHAPTER SEVEN

B ut unfortunately it was not so easy to convince the Inspector as it should have been. Indeed so firmly were his ideas fixed, that I had to use at last the argument which I hoped would be unnecessary. Also, I must freely admit, the course of the interview was frequently decided by him. I have no doubt that I could have prevented this, but I was hampered by the fact that I wished to be persuasive and therefore had to fall in with his desires to a larger extent than I should normally consider necessary.

"One of my difficulties, sir, in this matter," he said in reply to my reasoned request that he should abandon his theory of Miss Wyndham, "is that the account she gives me of the important afternoon is not entirely borne out by the very accurate statement which I have had the pleasure of taking down from you."

"The inaccuracy of the feminine mind, you know---" I suggested.

"Possibly, sir. Nevertheless I should like to check up with you the points where her statement differs."

With that, out came the inevitable notebook which I had come to look upon with some alarm as presaging a long and dreary interview. "In the first place she confirms Mr. Latimer's request that she should fetch the schedule of insertions in the *Daily Mail*. Also that such a request was usual at that time of day. Like you, sir, she considers that Mr. Latimer liked to be a nuisance. She ascribes it partly to a desire to show that he was important and partly to the general principle of desiring to cause inconvenience and friction."

"Then Miss Wyndham is a sounder psychologist than I thought. But you see how this bears out what I told you."

"Precisely. But she goes on to say that subsequently she heard no signs of any quarrel between the deceased."

"I think that I previously mentioned that conversation in any of the directors' rooms is not audible in the outer office. Besides she may have been typing herself, and the noise of that would drown any other sound."

"She says she was not doing so but was herself enjoying a short rest while taking her tea. She is very sure of that as she says it is her invariable custom to take a few minutes' break then. She says it is the only time in what she regards as an onerous day, that she does so."

"It is immaterial, but I hope Miss Wyndham will not induce you to believe she is hard worked. She is seldom asked to work overtime, for instance, or unduly hurried. But please go on."

Immaterial though it was, the Inspector thought it necessary to write it down. In future I should let such minor misapprehensions pass. "That would tend to confirm the statement that she was taking a short rest. Now I have carried out a few experiments, and while I agree that normal conversation in Mr. Latimer's room cannot be heard from where Miss Wyndham sits, raised voices can, if there is quiet outside."

"But was there quiet outside? Even if Miss Wyndham was not typing, she would certainly be chattering. Besides if Latimer was in his chair, Spencer would be standing with his back to the door, so that his voice would be going away from Miss Wyndham."

"Which, sir, brings me to the next point. It seems that Mr. Latimer allowed himself to be struck in the face extremely easily. Why should there have been no noise? Was there no struggle?"

"Very little," I answered.

Apparently the Inspector thought that he had induced me to make an answer without thinking. "And how do you know that?"

"Because this room is within earshot."

"Precisely, sir"—a pet adverb of the Inspector's—"but I want to know more about what you heard and why you did not interfere."

Quite why he did it I do not know, but obviously Hoopington had been leading up to this point and hoping that he would catch me unawares and get me to make some admission, which, I suppose, he hoped would help his case. As a matter of fact it was I who had been leading up to this point and I was delighted that apparently it had come from him. I had decided, in order to convince him that Spencer had been prepared to use violence against Latimer, to tell him the contents of what Spencer had written.

That it was actually written I thought it best to conceal, but I would inform him of the substance in a different way.

Accordingly I gave him quite a lengthy description of Spencer's fury over the Greyfields Canners and I said that he had *spoken* to me of his intention of telling Latimer exactly what he thought of him on that subject and on many others, and I ended by saying that Spencer had actually said that he intended to use force if necessary, but that anyhow Latimer should listen. "Return the black eye" were the actual words that he used to me. So that when I heard some slight disturbance I knew exactly what was happening and I saw no reason to interfere. "You see it had not then entered my head that Spencer would lose his temper to such an extent that he would in a fit of fury commit murder. Still less had it occurred to me that Latimer had worked himself up to such a state of hatred that he was intending to poison Spencer."

The Inspector looked at me rather coldly. "You should have mentioned this before."

It was time for me to turn the tables. "I think that that is hardly fair. I have now had the pleasure of several long interviews with you—very long if you will excuse my saying so—and I think you will admit that I have answered everything that you have asked me."

"But you have not before mentioned to me that you heard what must have been the actual struggle or that you had any reason to expect such a thing to happen. Come, sir, you ought not to have suppressed that!"

"On at least two occasions—if I may continue, Inspector—it has been on the tip of my tongue to tell you. But on both of those, as well as on others, you have seen fit to end the interview at a peculiar point. At least so it seemed to me."

"And those occasions were?"

"The first night. You dismissed the staff and said you wanted me to stay. Then, without assigning any reason for your action, you locked the door of my own room on me. Again, the other day you asked me some questions about my attitude to Miss Wyndham's marriage. Again it was on the tip of my tongue to tell you about this, but just as I was going to do so, you left."

Whatever other complaint I have to make about Inspector Hoopington, I must admit that he was perfectly fair. He was prepared at once to accept that as an adequate excuse. I must own I was surprised at how easily he was convinced, but then I suffered from the disadvantage that I knew that it was not entirely true. I had not in fact made up my mind until quite recently to describe what Spencer had written because I was afraid of in some way calling attention to the fact that it was not said, but was written. I am not an accomplished conspirator and I might say something stupid, might appear to know too much.

By now, too, I was convinced that I had made a mistake in keeping Spencer's notes away from the Inspector. They would have clinched the matter once and for all. I ought to have risked his being led astray by Spencer's foolish opinion of myself. If only Latimer had really written his diary in full, I think that I would have been glad to give Hoopington both!

Even as it was the Inspector was impressed. I think that something must be attributed to his pleasure in getting an account at all. It was, of course, very valuable evidence and, to my mind, quite conclusive. I had only kept it back partly for the reason that I have already given, partly because I hoped to prove my case without it, and partly because I was not sure whether it would merely be regarded as hearsay.

But now that it did come, the very fact that it had been apparently to some extent forced from me, made it doubly convincing. I was made to describe in great detail exactly what had been in theory said to me, which as I had read it through again quite recently, I was able to do quite easily.

Still, it took a long while, and when, halfway through, the Inspector came to the last page of his notebook, I conceived the childish hope that with the end of the book would come the end of taking notes. But the Inspector merely produced another book and went straight on. I believe if the end of the world were to come, he would appear before the Recording Angel with all the facts as to its dissolution neatly and unimaginatively tabulated.

However, at last the record was concluded, and I felt that I was going to be allowed to get on with my work. As it was, the advertisement for Flukil would have to remain unchanged, and though Fletcher, its owner, was a reasonable man who was prepared to make allowances for my difficulties, I was anxious to do everything that I could for him, but it was impossible to get Inspector Hoopington to see that work was more important than the solution of crime.

Perhaps though, it was merely that the solution of crime being work to him, he considered it important. At any rate he still desired to prolong the conversation.

"And that is all, sir? You have mentioned all Mr. Spencer's causes of complaint? Was there not something more in this street accident than the mere question of the ridicule attaching to a black eye and a rather infantile desire to inflict a similar pain?"

"Oh that," I answered readily enough. "I think there was really nothing in it, though at the time Spencer did seem to blame Latimer for carelessness in not warning him at once. Still, as I say, I think he really forgot all that and only remembered the eye. By the way, I suppose it was only a few minutes before he died that Latimer was hit?"

"We can of course tell that from the amount of discoloration. But as to Mr. Latimer's alleged carelessness over the car and Mr. Spencer's feelings of revenge– – –"

"Do you really want me to describe that?" I asked.

Apparently the Inspector did. More valuable minutes went by while many pages of the Inspector's new notebook were covered with his copy-book handwriting. I could not help noticing what a very uneconomic pattern of notebook it was. If I were allowed to reorganize the C.I.D., I am sure I could save the tax-payer a considerable sum under the heading of stationery alone. But then I am sure that if I were allowed to go through all the trifling extravagances of every Government Department and cut them down ruthlessly, it would reduce the income tax by at least sixpence in the pound. Look at the way they will telegraph instead of writing, for instance!

But it had been clever of me to have been apparently reluctant to mention that incident. Now that I did so, the Inspector lapped it down greedily. Direct methods having failed to convince him of the obvious truth, I had at last succeeded by catching him with what he thought was his own cleverness.

It was as well too that I had been quite ready to describe the incident in question, since apparently Hoopington had heard some rumour of it from the staff. In fact he must have been talking to them almost as much as to me. I do not think that, though I knew that he must have spoken to them, I had previously quite realized how much time he must have spent with each.

"Did not Mr. Spencer express some intention of writing an account of it?" he asked.

It was always possible for a reasonably intelligent person to guess what was in Hoopington's mind. When he adopted the particular tone in which he had addressed that question, I knew at once that he had been told that Spencer had talked of doing so, but that he rather hoped to trap me—though for what reason I could not think, except the general principle that if you can rattle anyone you can get anything out of him that you want. But I was too wary to be caught that way.

"I believe he did have some such idea. But Spencer was always going to do something, was always beginning things and not ending them. He was constantly rushing off in several directions at once and arriving nowhere as a result. In advertising, for instance, he would start to try to obtain half a dozen different clients at the same time, and through lack of concentration on any one, would fail to get any of them."

"You think then that he started to write this account and then stopped?"

"Possibly. Only if he had done so, wouldn't you have found it? Perhaps he never began it. Perhaps he began it and destroyed it. I think"—I adopted the attitude of one trying to recall to his memory a half-forgotten trivial detail—"that he did say something about having started it, so I presume he must have destroyed it. I fancy he found English composition rather difficult. But I am only guessing, Inspector."

"I quite understand. Precisely. The curious thing though, is that when Miss Wyndham took him his tea that afternoon she saw him writing. There were just three words at the top of the paper. She happened to notice them. They were 'I shall say.'"

"Yes, Inspector?"

"I have not found that piece of paper with that writing on it."

"Thrown away, I suppose. Spencer was always wasteful with stationery."

"I fancy, sir, that not everybody is as economical as you."

I smiled at the compliment while Hoopington went on. "But can you suggest where it went to? It was not in the waste-paper basket, and I am told that that had not been disturbed before I came—unless you moved anything, sir, by the way?"

"I? Why should I?"

"I thought not, sir, but I just asked."

How like Inspector Hoopington—he just asked! But I thought that it was advisable to give some explanation of the disappearance of the paper which was actually in my possession. "Possibly it would sound a fantastic explanation with anyone else, but with Spencer anything might happen—possibly he took a sudden dislike to it, crumpled it up, and threw it out of the window. That would be quite a typical action and I have seen him do it before. Besides, is there any reason to think that this paper which Miss Wyndham saw is the one to which you were referring?"

"None at all. And from what I hear of Mr. Spencer he might have done something like that. Only unfortunately it did not stay on the balcony underneath like the envelope. If only you had mentioned it at the time I could have had the area and the pavements searched."

"I should doubt whether you would have found it in a busy street, and even if you had, I cannot help wondering if it would have been any use to you."

"Very possibly, sir, but I like always to clear up every point."

As to that I believed the Inspector implicitly; I had had too much proof of it already. But I was interested in his reference to the envelope on the balcony; which I had been meaning to ask him about before. However I did so then.

"Oh, yes, that is quite an interesting feature. It had contained the poison."

"Then I suppose it was used as a container by Latimer for the crystals he took from my drawer?"

"That seems to me, sir, to assume a great many things."

"I think, though, that I may say that it confirms the account I have already given you of what happened."

"Of what you think happened, sir, if I may correct you," was his annoying reply. "It still has not been proved, and I might say that I have other theories. Murder, you know, sir, is not easy. Nor is the solution of it always as simple as you appear to think."

How like Inspector Hoopington! Of course I was certain that I had guessed correctly what his theory was (and equally sure that theory was wrong) but it did not seem apparently to occur to him that I might have read his thoughts and he refused to say openly what his ideas were. I, as a mere layman not having the privilege of being in Scotland Yard, however much I might know and however much I might actually assist, must be kept at arm's length, lest I should be able to claim any credit for having assisted the police! An interesting if a narrow attitude.

Busy though I was, I found this all so intriguing that I made rather full notes on it almost at once.

CHAPTER EIGHT

Time passes quickly when one is busy and it was only the periodical adjournments of the coroner's inquest which called my attention to the dilatoriness of Scotland Yard.

NeO-aD was really busy too. My Galatz-si campaign was being a great success and, in addition, I had no difficulty in getting all the press publicity that I wanted. When the first sensational paragraphs as to 'Double Tragedy in Advertising Agents' Office' came out, I had of course taken care to see that the press were supplied with the fullest details about the company and its capabilities and also the fact that business would in no way be impeded. Our clients, though none of them sufficiently big to be really well known, were numerous, and the list I was able to supply was quite imposing.

The next stage was to let it be known that the 'tragedy' had been caused by a new product which we were putting on the market. This required rather careful handling because although publicity was to be had in plenty, it was very important not to allow the impression to be stamped on the public mind that Galatz-si was dangerous. But I have always found that if you handle them the right way, the press are very helpful and of course they especially wish to be so to an advertising agent since it is we who decide in which of them our clients are going to buy space.

With therefore interesting news to tell them and a promise that an advertising campaign was about to be started almost in connection with it, I had the press at my feet. Indeed many free columns were devoted to Galatz-si before I bought an inch of space. It was a great temptation to charge Tonescu with the price of some of them at advertising rates—particularly some of the accounts of the coroner's enquiry, when I managed to discuss the product in great detail.

But I thought it was not right to take advantage of his ignorance. In the end I contented myself with adding a sum for publicity work. He accepted it so readily that I wished I had asked for double the amount.

When the notoriety gained by the police proceedings was reinforced by the advertising, Tonescu readily obtained magnificent sales. He took offices, raised the price per tin, and accepted my suggestion to extend his campaign to several others of the London dailies. What with the success that he was having and the attention which both that success and the inquest was calling to the agency, I could see a long and prosperous future before me.

The more I contemplated Latimer's and Spencer's departure, the more I appreciated the truth of the old adage about ill winds— and the beauty of it was that, under the terms of our agreement, I had been able to buy their interest for next to nothing. Galatz-si had helped me but not them. So great was the success that I was even able to look with equanimity on Latimer's account which showed a small balance due to me which would never be paid.

Thinking the matter over, I came to the conclusion that it would be advisable to get a better artist and a better typist— possibly I should need two typists.

At this time, too, I decided to move into the room which Latimer had occupied, which I need hardly say was the best—

Latimer might have been trusted to obtain that. Thomas also, I prepared to move, very much against his will, into what had been Spencer's room. He would be able to work there with no disturbance. My own would be used for a second typist or perhaps for someone who would interview the press representatives for me—a tiresome and rather useless job which took up a great deal of time. At any rate for the present I left it unoccupied.

Thomas was rather troublesome about the move. I thought at first that he merely objected because he was used to being in one place and did not want to change. As for the excuse that he put up, it was palpably absurd. He said that he disliked sitting in a room where anyone had died. He even pretended that his artistic temperament made him psychic and that he expected to see a ghost! That of course was nonsense. Thomas was a second-class commercial designer—good enough, when we could not afford anyone better, but nothing more than that and no more artistic than a black-beetle.

Of course his real reason was that he did not want to be separated from dear Maud, but at the time it had never entered my head that they were married.

As, however, his objections developed into passive disobedience, and then into open refusal, the real reason suddenly dawned on me, and with a flash of intuition, I accused him of being engaged to Miss Wyndham. His hesitation before saying 'No' gave him away, and put into my head the idea of asking if they were married.

Once that fact was known the whole situation changed. Of course I made up my mind to dismiss them both at the earliest opportunity. I could not put my reasons so crudely as Spencer, nor are they exactly the same, but I am sure that a married woman's heart is not in her work and I would have no one in my office who was not wholly devoted to what she was doing. I had for some time been thinking of getting rid of her and this piece of news finally decided it. With her, Thomas would naturally have to go. Apart from anything else, he would be impossible when I had dismissed her.

I came to this decision very easily, but I was prudent enough not to tell them until I had engaged successors. Those who are under notice to go are always lazy—perhaps it is natural. It would be well worth while to delay telling them of my intention until I actually had successors coming the next day.

The only question was whether I should have to pay them a month's wages in lieu of notice or whether a week would be sufficient. Rather reluctantly I came to the conclusion that a month would be necessary. Even though Galatz-si was bringing in a considerable amount of income to me, I saw no reason to be wasteful. I should try to see if an offer of a fortnight's wages would not be sufficient.

I have had some difficulty in selecting those who are to take their places without either of them having any idea of my intentions, but I think I have managed it. The dismissal will take place on the day following what I hope will be the final adjournment of the inquest. There will, of course, be no trial if Hoopington has the intelligence to accept the obvious view of the situation which I have put before him. If, on the other hand, he is anxious to prosecute the Thomases, he can do so for all I care. They will no longer be in my employment. Indeed it would perhaps be as well if I were to have dismissed them before they were arrested.

Accordingly, therefore, the next time I saw the Inspector I rather changed my tone. I took the attitude that perhaps I had been wrong in pressing my own view so strongly upon him. Then I went on to say that I was sure that he had formed the theory that Thomas and Miss Wyndham were responsible, and that though I thought that they were not, I had no desire to impede justice in any way.

"By the way," I went on, "did you know that they were married to each other?"

Now I had hoped that this was a fresh fact to the Inspector—it is a pardonable piece of vanity, I hope, but, in common with many other people, I like my news to *be* news.

It was therefore rather depressing to find that the Inspector had known it all the time. I upbraided him with having concealed it from me and pointed out that it was very material to me that I should know it. In return I got a rather guarded account of how he had found out the fact, from which, drawing, I must admit, slightly on my imagination, I have described the rencontre with Mrs. Wyndham.

At the end, however, he reverted to my comment that it was so intimately a concern of mine that he ought to have told me. He had not, he said, when he had discussed it with me, realized that I felt in any way so strongly about it. Indeed he seemed quite upset when I explained to him that I had made full arrangements to get rid of both of them.

The information had one unexpected consequence, which makes me doubt Inspector Hoopington's veracity and sincerity.

He instantly dropped the theory to which I am sure he had been working up, that the Thomases were in any way responsible. Indeed he had the audacity to pretend that he had never contemplated such a possibility and went so far as to say that he had really come to the conclusion that I had been right all the time and that he hoped to satisfy the coroner fully as to that.

I was in reality delighted to hear it. Such a conclusion would settle the matter once and for all, since if the police believed that each murdered the other and the coroner's jury brought in a verdict to that effect, there could be no subsequent trial, there being nobody to try. But, having by now learned that Inspector Hoopington moved by contraries, I naturally did not say so. Instead I pressed him to make certain that Thomas had not poisoned Latimer while Miss Wyndham poisoned Spencer's tea.

"In which case, sir, you listened to Mr. Spencer talking to Mr. Latimer after Miss Wyndham had killed him."

I pretended to consider this seriously. "Unless I mistook Thomas's voice for Spencer's."

"But you heard his voice, I thought, and you heard him go from his room to Mr. Latimer's."

"That might have been Miss Wyndham moving about. And I did not hear the voices very distinctly."

My tactics worked admirably. Inspector Hoopington, though obviously by now completely muddled, only saw safety in sticking to the point to which I wanted him to adhere, namely the double murder.

"The black eye alone, sir, I think is conclusive." Well, I had always thought so but it had taken Inspector Hoopington a long while to arrive at the conclusion!

Finally he came back rather unexpectedly to the envelope which had been found on the balcony below. "I think that that is a point which, though not decisive, is rather in Miss Wyndham's favour. It is practically certain that since it contained traces of Galatz-si, it had been used as a container for the portion taken out of your stock. Therefore it was used by the murderer or one of the murderers, who would want to dispose of it as quickly as possible."

I agreed fairly readily. I was hoping that the Inspector would see that this was Latimer's doing, but I was anxious not to press it too hard.

"Now Miss Wyndham could have dropped such an envelope out of the window of her own room much more easily, or quite simply could have torn it up and put it into the very full waste-paper basket in her room. She would not have suspected me of having the whole of its contents examined."

"Which you did?"

"Naturally. But Mr. Latimer would have wanted to get rid of it at once. Therefore it went out of his own window without delay. That it should catch on the balcony below was pure bad luck which he had left out of his calculations."

This train of reasoning seemed to me to be based on very slender premises and to be composed of facts which did not follow necessarily from each other.

I was anxious that the Inspector should accept it as accurate, but I hoped he would not bring it forward openly. Even a coroner's jury might fail to find it convincing. Accordingly, partly as a warning and partly to conceal my real desire, I argued against it. But it was no good trying to convince Hoopington. The more I said the more determined he became.

At any rate I had achieved my principal object. When the final adjournment of the inquest is held, there is no doubt what theory Hoopington will produce. And of course I shall adjust my evidence so as to bear it out fully. Indeed there will be no need to 'adjust'. It will bring it out fully naturally.

CHAPTER NINE

One more note and my task will be ended.

The coroner's inquest has gone off admirably and the whole thing is finished and may be dismissed from my mind. When these last few words are written—and they are only written because I am not happy unless I have rounded off my work—I shall be quite free to concentrate on the work before me.

I shall not describe the inquest in detail. It was, I presume, much as all others. On the previous occasions nothing but formal evidence had been given, but now that at long last Inspector Hoopington had completed his laborious investigations and had arrived at the point which I had reached many weeks before, I was asked to tell the full story.

It was to some extent in anticipation of this moment that I had carefully compiled this chronicle, so that I was able to give a very full account, not only of everything that had happened on what the press called 'the fatal afternoon', but also of the attitudes and feelings of all concerned.

Indeed I think I may say that mine was the only evidence of any moment whatever.

I was able to show convincingly how Spencer and Latimer

grated on each other and how both considered the other to be incompetent. I took care not to blacken their abilities too deeply since I had no wish to tell the world that NeO-aD (I am wondering by the way whether to change the name to something less foolish) was not competent. All the same a careful reader would see that the essential man in the agency was myself, and I, of course, still remain.

Nor did I neglect the interest of our clients. Both Henriques and Fletcher received a useful 'puff' and the subscription list for the shares of Greyfields Canners, when it comes out, will be the more easily subscribed since its name and objects will be known. All these three really owe me something for my efforts on their behalf but, unlike Tonescu, I doubt if they will consent to pay it. There is a certain amount of prejudice, I find, against taking advantage of such an opportunity and Fletcher of Flukil, in particular, was a friend of Spencer's and is grieved at his death and seems to think that I should be too. In fact he has almost reproached me for a want of feeling, which is absurd.

When we came to the question of the afternoon on which they died and of what had actually happened, I had little difficulty. I had already shown the probability of their desiring to kill each other. It remained only to show the possibility and the method used.

Fortunately the procedure of a coroner's court allows of ample latitude, the advantage of which I had never before realized, which indeed I had been apt to condemn, and so I was able to express my whole theory to them. It was, I think, fortunate for the coroner, otherwise Hoopington would have had to have explained, and I doubt whether he was capable of doing so.

In any case it would certainly have taken longer and not been so clear and convincing. Besides he would have confined himself to facts, whereas I allowed myself to indulge in speculation. It took a long time, but in a necessary cause I never grudge work.

After my evidence there was little more to be done. Hoopington was called, but he contented himself with confirming parts of my story and leaving the rest uncorroborated but unshaken. As a formality Thomas and his wife were both put in the box but they only succeeded in causing a slight confusion. Even allowing for the necessary formal witnesses, I was examined for a longer period than the rest put together.

Of course the jury could only come to the right conclusion— that Spencer and Latimer had murdered each other. I really forget whether they said they were temporarily insane or not. It is not of the slightest importance.

So then the whole thing is settled and over, and it only remains to tell that incompetent pair of their dismissal. I shall do it with particular relish as Miss Wyndham, or rather Mrs. Thomas, had the effrontery to contradict at the inquest one of my statements, namely, that a door in the directors' part of the office had been opened once after she had taken round the tea and before she found Latimer's body.

Yes, I shall part with the Thomases, and with them all recollection of the affair, with the greatest pleasure.

PART IV
EXECUTION

CHAPTER ONE

I shall not start by making an unkind remark like Mr. Barraclough, although there are many things that I might say. But what I have always said is that I do think that it is up to any secretary to know all about the man she is managing. I mean I do not think that he ought to have any secrets really from her as far as his business is concerned. Of course, his private life is another matter.

Now there are a lot of things that a girl ought to know which perhaps it is not quite easy for her to be told. Well, anyone with a little imagination can see that. So I have always said that the proper thing to do is to find out, ever so quietly of course, and then one just knows without having to be told. That's just good business sense, and I don't think needs any apologies. Of course lots of girls think differently, I know. They think you ought never to look at anything, but I don't agree.

Anyhow, right or wrong, that's what my idea is, and that's why when I saw Mr. Spencer writing away, I wanted to know what it was all about. But as Mr. Barraclough has said, all I saw was three words at the top of the page—'I shall say', and that didn't tell me much, although afterwards it did seem to point to his being going to talk to Mr. Latimer, at least, that's how Mr. Barraclough made it out, though at the time I didn't really know quite what to think. It made me quite worried that I did not know what else he had said.

And so, when I found the drawer of Mr. Barraclough's table unlocked at last and a long manuscript in it, of course I looked. Well, naturally any good secretary would. It might have been something that I ought to be typing. And when I saw that it ended up that he said he was going to part with me and Percy with the greatest pleasure, I was glad I had. You see, up to that minute, I had never thought of losing my post with NeO-aD; there was no reason why I should—it wasn't as if I wasn't doing the work properly—and it did come as a nasty shock. And as for anyone being glad to get rid of Percy, well, that I could *not* understand!

Of course, there were plenty of other positions I could get, and Percy could command his figure anywhere, being a really clever artist, and there aren't so many of them, but still, even though we were paid shockingly little by Mr. Barraclough, it was a job, and it always takes a few weeks to find another place, and if Mr. Barraclough could think of dismissing us like that, he might not give me so good a reference as he ought to.

So what with one thing and another, and the instalments due on the hire purchase of the furniture, I thought something ought to be done about it.

Well, Mr. Barraclough had been disturbed that morning and was in an awful state—I shall come to that soon—and there would be a little while before he came back, so I thought there was time to look at this paper of his a little more carefully.

I wondered why I had not seen it before, for one thing, because I was sure it had not been in the office before, unless he kept it locked up, which was a mean trick he had to prevent me seeing things, but when I read a bit of it, I wondered how he had come to leave it about at all.

Then I saw that he had meant to lock the drawer but being so dreadfully flurried he had turned the catch before it was quite shut, and that a careful man like him should do a thing like that only just showed how upset he was.

Of course there had been a nasty business that morning, but it all seemed to be over, even if he had had to pay to get rid of the woman, and then he had telephoned to that Rumanian—at least he says he is a Rumanian, but Percy doesn't believe he is—I shall come to that, too, soon—and I couldn't quite hear what he said, because I don't like to let the office boy see me listening in, it doesn't seem dignified, but anyhow, he had run out in an awful stew, and I suppose he must have been terribly excited, or he wouldn't ever have left it lying about, not even in the drawer.

Naturally I turned back to the beginning and started reading, and I got puzzled at once. It was half of it in Mr. Barraclough's handwriting, but there were bits of it in Mr. Latimer's, and of course actually Mr. Barraclough had written most of it himself, but after I read a bit I saw the words—'got hold of Barraclough', and that did not make sense if Mr. Barraclough was writing it himself. After a bit I saw that it was all supposed to be written by Mr. Latimer, and that made it funnier than ever.

So then I made up my mind to take it away and look at it fully. You see, I had seen that he was going to dismiss us without having any reason, and I knew perhaps I was giving him an excuse, but I couldn't help that. Having these papers might make him change his mind, or at any rate we might be able to get better compensation for being sent away so suddenly, and at any rate he should not have it back until he wrote us both a proper reference.

Just at that moment, too, I happened to see that he thought he ought to give us a month's wages, but was going to try to get off with less. Well, that was just like his meanness! I took it across and showed it to Percy.

Percy's clever—oh, he is ever so clever! He saw at once that the first part was mainly written by Mr. Barraclough pretending to be

Mr. Latimer and sticking in bits that Mr. Latimer had put in a diary.

"Why," he said, "this is just Barraclough's way of writing. No one who knew Latimer would ever have thought that this was written by him."

"Well, I must say," I answered, "I never should have thought Mr. Latimer would have taken all that trouble."

"Nor given himself away so." Of course, directly Percy said that, I saw how true it was.

Now that I have had time to read it over quietly I can see, too, how right Percy was when he said it wasn't written at all in the way Mr. Latimer put things, and I ought to know, having taken down all their letters for years. When later on I came across the bit where Mr. Barraclough says that he prides himself on having written it just like Mr. Latimer, I fairly laughed out loud, I did really. But all that comes later.

The next thing that happened was that Percy came across several sheets of it written in Mr. Spencer's handwriting, and ending up—'I shall say!'.

Well, that was a surprise! Here was the paper which I had always said I had seen and which Mr. Barraclough had told the Inspector that he thought Mr. Spencer had thrown out of the window, and here it was all the time.

"Well, would you ever believe it!" I said to Percy.

He seemed quite excited too.

"I think you know, old girl"—I loved his calling me 'old girl'—"that we ought to telephone to Hoopington." Just quietly, like that! As if telephoning to Scotland Yard was quite an ordinary thing to do! I couldn't help being ever so proud of Percy.

But I didn't let on just then. It doesn't do for a girl to let her husband know always how proud she is of him, so I just thought 'I'll show I'm worthy of you', and without letting him see how thrilled I was, I just picked up the receiver and dialed as if it were an ordinary number.

Percy told me afterwards that there wasn't a tremor in my voice when I asked for Mr. Hoopington, and when I told him we had got what Mr. Spencer wrote, I could hear at once that he was excited too, although he never was one to show much what he was feeling. He said he would come round at once.

But before I say a word more, now that I have read all that Mr. Barraclough has written, let me put one or two things right.

First of all about Mother. I shall never forgive Mr. Barraclough for what he said about mother, never. Mother never talked that way. Why, you might think from what he says, that she stood gossiping on the doorstep like I don't know what. Mother wouldn't ever do a thing like that. She's much too well-bred. I mean she is a very refined lady, and if it did happen to slip out when she was talking to the Inspector that I was married, well, why shouldn't she say so? There was no secret about that, except that we didn't think it was advisable to mention it in the office.

I should like now to say why we hadn't told everyone. First of all Mr. Spencer would have his joke. Now I liked Mr. Spencer, but you never knew what he wouldn't say next, and I must admit that I was rather afraid of what sort of jokes he would make. Mr. Spencer was always the gentleman, but I must say sometimes he thought things were funny which I thought were just the smallest trifle vulgar, but then, there's no accounting for tastes, and well-brought up gentlemen like Mr. Spencer often have got a much lower standard than we have. I've never met a lord, but I shouldn't be surprised if he were downright common.

But it wasn't so much Mr. Spencer's jokes that we were afraid of, as the other two. First of all there was Mr. Latimer, and you never could tell what *he* wouldn't do.

Stuck-up pig, he was! Generally said very little, but when he did it was rude. I never could abide him, though Percy always said he was all right if you took him the right way, but I never found out what the way was, and even Percy was annoyed with him when he tore up those drawings for the Canning Company. Oh, they were ever so lovely! You could hardly believe how lovely they were!

Still the main difficulty really we felt would be Mr. Barraclough. Percy always said that he was so mean that he would say we wouldn't work well if we were married, and you see Percy was quite right. But then Percy always is.

So you see Mr. Barraclough has given quite a wrong explanation as to why we said nothing and as to what people were like.

He was quite wrong, too, about the Inspector. Mr. Hoopington and I were great friends. I am sure he never would have thought for a moment that Percy and I could have done such a thing as Mr. Barraclough says Mr. Hoopington thought we might have done to Mr. Spencer and Mr. Latimer. Oh, dear, it is so involved! But anyhow, Mr. Hoopington is not that sort of man. He was always so quiet and kind. I looked on him quite like a father! And then he was so big and strong, and really rather good-looking, and ever so patient and gentle. I had a lot of long talks with him, and whatever Mr. Barraclough may say about what the Coroner thought, I know Mr. Hoopington thought a lot of what I said. He took it all down most carefully, and I could see he considered it most important. And so in the end it was—but I shall come to that later.

Mother liked him very much too, by the way. All that bit about her saying that he wasn't a gentleman is most misleading. Well, you may let a word slip out edge-wise occasionally, and Mr. Hoopington did look better than an ordinary policeman, and of course he was. But he and mother got on beautifully. We went back that night to where I lived because he wanted to talk to Percy too, but that was the only reason.

And as for saying that Mr. Hoopington was angry with her, and so tried to fasten things on to us, why, he wouldn't demean himself that way. Besides he wasn't angry and he always knew we had nothing to do with it. I always felt that one could say whatever one wanted to him; besides, he had such a way with him that almost anyone would talk, even mother who is usually a most *silent* person. But when Mr. Hoopington is with one, one does get talking so!

So you see nearly everything Mr. Barraclough has said is wrong. But perhaps what is most unfair is when he said I didn't work hard, and why he wanted to go on harping about my teeth I don't know. If he had been a gentleman he wouldn't have noticed them, but Mr. Spencer was the only one who was that, and didn't the others just hate him if he reminded them about his education! Well, he could be a bit annoying, but still. ...

But to go back to me and my work. I should like to say that no girl could have worked harder than I did. There sharp at eight-forty-five in the morning, and never later than nine, and if I was, I always found Mr. Barraclough there before me and being sarcastic. And barely getting three-quarters of an hour for lunch and not leaving till after half-past six and often seven, and even later, and not getting any extra money for it, so that when Mr. Barraclough said, as he did to Mr. Hoopington, that I never did any overtime, it would have been more truthful to have said that I was not paid for any overtime. Well, really, it was something cruel.

Percy often spoke to me about it.

"Maud," he said, "Maud, you'll wear yourself out if you go on like that."

"Well," I said, "what can one do? What with the shorthand and the typing for three people, and a little for you too, dear, sometimes, though I know you can't help it, and then all the filing—well, someone's got to do it."

"There ought to be two people. You're doing the work of two, Maud."

"Well, and look how much you're doing, dear! But I must say if someone would do the typing of all these accounts and estimates and schedules and the figures, I won't say I wouldn't be glad. Figures do take such a time to type."

"I shall talk to Barraclough myself to-morrow."

Percy was so brave that I thought he would, and I know Mr. Barraclough would never have done it. Why, even when all that Galatz-si work had to be done, he only *thought* of getting a second girl. But he didn't do it. So I made Percy promise. "Don't you ever do such a thing without my consent," I said. And of course Percy said he wouldn't. You can always trust Percy.

But that reminds me of these two things at least that I was going to come to later, and one was Galatz-si. Well, in a way, they were both Galatz-si, and I think I'll take the other one first. Like Mr. Barraclough I'll stop and put a 'Fig. II' and start again. I mean I suppose that's right and I ought to do things properly now that I have begun to go in for literature.

CHAPTER TWO

Well, the other one is what happened first this morning, and most unpleasant it was just at first. Though afterwards I did have a bit of a laugh, and then things really did begin happening.

Very soon after I got in, an elderly person came in at the door and asked if this was NeO-aD. I said it was.

"Where the late Mr. Spencer used to work?" she asked.

I said "yes" of course. Quite a respectable looking person she was, with a bit of a cast in her left eye and a habit of folding her arms about her chest. But rather quarrelsome, I should think. I didn't take to her exactly.

"I was his landlady," she said. "He had my best room and I'll trouble you, young lady, to let me see whoever owns this business now, because compensation I will have or my name's not Mrs. Higgins."

"Compensation for what?" I said.

"That's my business," she says, really rude like.

Well, I don't like being taken up like that. No one would like it. So I thought I had better be a bit haughty myself.

"Mr. Barraclough is a very busy man," I told her, "and he never likes being disturbed unless it is something really important. I am his confidential secretary," I went on, "and if I can assist you in any way---"

"You can assist me, young woman, by letting me see this Mr. Barraclough, and pretty quick too."

"If you would be so good as to tell me what the matter is I will ascertain if Mr. Barraclough is disengaged. Probably he will make an appointment with you for some other date." I should have liked to have produced a diary and allotted her something like three o'clock on the following Thursday week, but Mr. Barraclough never would let me make his appointments for him.

At that, Mrs. Higgins tapped her elbows with her bony fingers and gave a little stamp.

"I see your Mr. Barraclough this morning and I do not leave this office until I have seen him, and you may take that as quite final."

Well, there was nothing else to do, so I told her that I would enquire what Mr. Barraclough's wishes were. If I could manage it, she should be kept waiting some time. Well, I usually try to help people, but this Mrs. Higgins annoyed me. Just as I was going she condescended to explain her business a little.

"You can tell him." she said, "that I've come about my mirror."

I didn't really like delivering that message to Mr. Barraclough. It was so vague. He was often rather cross in the mornings, but there it was, there was nothing else to do. But, to my surprise, he seemed quite interested. I had to show Mrs. Higgins in at once, and I didn't like the triumphant look she gave me, as much as to say:

"There, you've had to do it after all, you see."

Just as I shut the door behind her I remembered that it was on a mirror that Mr. Spencer had experimented with Galatz-si, and of course I ought to know all about what happened to it. So I just waited quietly in the passage and listened.

Well, there was a terrible row. It seemed that Mr. Spencer had put the stuff on too thick, which is just what Mr. Spencer would have done, and the result was that it had damaged the glass, eaten it away, Mrs. Higgins said, so that it was no good any longer as a mirror and was getting rapidly worse.

"It started with just one or two queer spots a few days ago and now all one corner has rotted away completely; that's the corner where he rubbed this stuff on."

"Are you sure?" Mr. Barraclough had said.

"Quite. He had the impertinence to do it without telling me, but he did have the goodness to mention it afterwards. Quite proud, he was, of the way the steam would not settle on it—the saucy man. And his jokes about my being able to have the water hot in future, whereas it is always hot enough, except for a sala- mander. But that Mr. Spencer was always making silly remarks like that, even to me. He knew well enough I did not appreciate them."

"I really do not know that I can accept that," I heard Mr. Barra- clough reply. "There might be many other reasons why the mirror has decayed."

"None," snapped Mrs. Higgins. "And I'll tell you another thing which proves it. He said he had upset a few drops on another part of the mirror, and that's beginning to go too. Right down vicious stuff it must be. If it eats into your inside like it does into my glass, no wonder he and the other gentleman here died quickly."

I must admit I was rather enjoying this, even though the last remark was a bit gruesome. It was quite unusual to hear Mr. Barr- aclough being put down like this. I only wished that I could see his face. Eventually however he got a word in.

"I am sorry to hear of the damage to your mirror, but what has it to do with me? Except that I am very much obliged to you for telling me. I am afraid that Mr. Spencer must have used too strong a solution."

"What's it got to do with you, young man? You or your company are going to pay for it."

I very nearly gave myself away by laughing out loud. We all knew very well how very much Mr. Barraclough disliked paying for anything. Quite what he said I don't know, but I think he said that any mistake that Mr. Spencer made, concerned him alone and that she had better apply to his executors.

But Mrs. Higgins was not so easily disposed of.

"Stuff and nonsense," she said. "He did it because you told him to, as part of the company, and the company is liable. I'm not leaving here until I am paid."

I could not help wondering if Mrs. Higgins's rather large black bag contained her dinner. She seemed quite determined to spend a long while with us, and really I think she would have carried out her threat. But whether she would or not I never found out as Mr. Barraclough made what was probably a mistake—or perhaps it was the best thing he could do. He offered her a pound as compensation, carefully saying that he did not admit liability.

"A pound, young man! Do you think I can buy another one for that? I believe it cost my dear husband over twenty, but I'll take fifteen!"

Now I don't believe that either of them had the slightest idea of what a mirror of that size did cost, and I know I did not, but I have always thought that there were mirrors and mirrors, and that a good deal depended on the frame, but I may be wrong.

Anyhow, they started bargaining and if they didn't know much about mirrors, they both knew a good deal about haggling. I think that if they ever met again, which of course they won't, that Mr. Barraclough would win, but as it was, he was at a disadvantage because he did not want to waste time. Eventually they agreed at eight pounds five shillings, which is five shillings more than half the difference, between the pound Mr. Barraclough offered and the fifteen pounds she wanted—at least it isn't but that's how she worked it out.

Even then there was a dispute about whether it should be a cheque or cash. But that argument Mrs. Higgins was bound to lose because we never keep much petty cash in the office, so I did not wait for the end of that but hurried back to my own desk just in time to hear Mrs. Higgins leave and find Mr. Barraclough ringing through to tell me to get him M. Tonescu on the telephone.

Soon afterwards he ran off without saying where he was going, which was most unusual, and I went in to tidy his papers and found the manuscript.

In the excitement of that I forgot to tell Percy what I had heard, but before Mr. Hoopington reached us, I did just mention it. It was then that Percy told me one of the other things that I said I would mention later. He said at once:

"Take it from me, old girl, we're going to find out that this Tonescu is a rotter in some way or other."

"Why, whatever makes you say that?" I asked.

"Well, do you remember the first day he came here he got excited and talked in Rumanian? Well, I thought at the time it wasn't, because I recognized a few words and they were Welsh. You know I learnt just a little so that I could pretend I'm a Welshman for a joke, because of my name? Well, I can't talk enough to follow everything people say, but I believe he was talking Welsh and pretending it was Rumanian—so I'm sure we shall find out all the rest of him was a sham."

"Oh, but Percy, oughtn't you to have said so?"

On that he turned on me almost angry—it's the only time I've known him be.

"Well, I wasn't sure. And a fine lot of loyalty you and I owe to this concern! Besides, perhaps there may be some words the same in both, like English and Latin."

Well, of course, I saw all that at once.

But afterwards, when the whole thing came out, it was proved that Percy was quite right all the time. It seems that M. Tonescu was not a Rumanian at all, but a Welshman called Tony something, Williams, I think, and that the stuff wasn't made at Galatz at all—for all I know, there isn't such a place—but that he had it done up by someone else who was in the swindle with him somewhere in Hoxton and that they both knew quite well that in time it would destroy any glass that it was put on to.

Apparently he pretended to be a Rumanian so as to play a sort of confidence trick on Mr. Latimer. I think he must have overheard Mr. Latimer say at the Exhibition just before he first met him that he was an advertising agent, perhaps say something about providing capital, and so have wanted to pretend to meet him by chance and to be very ignorant, and to be ready to do whatever he was told. (All that part of the diary was really Mr. Latimer's, of course.)

Anyhow, thinking that he was just a stupid foreigner, even Mr. Barraclough had not taken him seriously, although they had all taken the product seriously, and so they had not found out enough about him, and he had been able to be vague and get away with all sorts of things. I heard afterwards, too, that the Rumanian bank reference was forged, and I suppose it would be easier to do that than to forge an English one. Well, everyone knows that the banks abroad aren't the same as ours.

Of course, until Mr. Barraclough came back, I did not realize quite how serious it all was. But I could see that it did matter, because if Galatz-si was going to eat into Mrs. Higgins's mirror, perhaps it would eat into all other glass, unless of course Mr. Barraclough was right when he said that Mr. Spencer had used too strong a solution.

That, of course, was the first thing that he thought of too. After he had telephoned to M. Tonescu (and how much he said to him I don't know), he went straight off, so I heard afterwards, to look at his own car. As it happened he hadn't used it for several days, perhaps weeks, and he wanted naturally to look at the windscreen.

And when he did see it and found that it was beginning to go wrong too, sort of mouldy-like, it must have been an awful shock, because of course that meant that all the rest would go soon, too, and then goodness knows what would happen. I suppose Tonescu's company would have had to replace them all if they had got the money, but whether NeO-aD were liable, too, I never really did find out. At any rate we had made a great reputation with Galatz-si, and if that was going to turn out to be no good after all, it would be bound to do us a great deal of harm. Sort of reaction, you know.

But all this was just thinking about what the future might be, and as a matter of fact it hardly mattered at all amongst so many other things which all happened that day. Because while Mr. Barraclough was looking at his car, and I suppose going on to see M. Tonescu, Mr. Hoopington arrived.

Well, neither Percy nor I wanted to talk to him in front of the office boys. Those lads were supposed chiefly to go and fetch voucher copies of papers and magazines ('books' as we call them in the advertising profession) and make themselves useful generally, which they seldom were. They were always out when they were wanted, and in when they weren't.

So of course now they were in. Now I think Mr. Barraclough has said that he had moved into what was Mr. Latimer's room and that his old room was empty. So Percy and I took Mr. Hoopington into there, and there we showed him what we had found.

CHAPTER THREE

W ell, of course he was very interested. He said he would like to read it all through, but of course there wasn't time then, and anyhow Mr. Barraclough had a shocking small handwriting which I always have said is the mark of a mean man. Mr. Latimer's wasn't too easy to read, as well I knew, though he did generally dictate, as causing more trouble, so we just showed him that there was a bit written by Mr. Spencer, and that it was what he was writing just before he died, and I also just mentioned what nasty ideas Mr. Barraclough had had about us.

Mr. Hoopington said that that was the final piece of evidence for which he had been waiting, and then he began to outline to us what his theory had really been all the time. Actually he wasn't able to tell us everything just then because of course he hadn't long, but because we had helped him—and for one other reason which I shall mention later—he promised to tell us all about it afterwards, and I must say I think that was ever so good of him. So, later on he filled in all the details besides those which became quite public property soon after.

He told us that the first thing which had seemed curious to

him was when Mr. Barraclough saw the envelope on the balcony below. It seemed to him funny that it should have stuck there.

Then he looked for finger marks on the window of Mr. Latimer's room, and there weren't any, whereas there were plenty of Mr. Barraclough's on his window sash. Still, that was natural enough and quite possible, and Mr. Barraclough said he had opened his window during the afternoon. All the same, Mr. Hoopington thought it was funny that Mr. Barraclough should so definitely call attention to the envelope, especially as it seemed to be more under his window than Mr. Latimer's.

So he changed his mind and decided not to go on questioning Mr. Barraclough that night, but to get rid of him at once and experiment. He found that he had difficulty in getting any envelope to lodge on the balcony, and it would not go there except from Mr. Barraclough's room.

Now, Mr. Hoopington was always fair and he never liked rushing things, so he didn't jump to any conclusions from that, but he saw which way it pointed, and when he went down to the street below and found another exactly similar envelope, also with traces of Galatz-si, he was almost sure that he knew what had happened.

You see, that pointed to someone having failed to get the envelope to stay at the first shot. So someone wanted him to find that envelope—in other words it was a false clue deliberately laid, and it was Mr. Barraclough who called attention to it.

Directly Mr. Hoopington had seen that, the whole thing got a lot clearer, and after he had been out to our home, it was plainer still, because I told him how I took round the tea and he saw that Mr. Barraclough could have put the poison in both their teas before it ever reached Mr. Latimer!

Well, I must say he must have done it under my nose, and I don't now remember anything suspicious; perhaps he did it while he was taking sugar, I do remember a bit of fumbling then, I think. Well, anyhow, that must have been it, and then just as Mr. Latimer was dying, he went in and hit him in the face and scattered the crystals about just to make it look like what he was writing, and I must say he must have had a nerve to do that, besides it not being at all a nice thing to do to go hitting a dying man like that.

At first I couldn't think why he wanted to do it but Mr. Hoopington made that clear to me. Of course it was just to throw suspicion on Mr. Spencer because of the accident that had happened to him. But really there Mr. Barraclough was a bit too clever, which serves him right, because it seems that he had to hit him while he was still alive or else his eye wouldn't bruise properly. It's not the sort of thing that a girl likes talking about and I really do apologize for putting it in, but one must say everything, even if it is gruesome, but it seems that the amount of discoloration was so slight that allowing for the time that the poison would take to act, it ought to have been more, because I think Mr. Hoopington said (though I don't quite understand) that after you are dead, you don't bruise.

Oh, and Mr. Hoopington thinks that Mr. Barraclough thought of pretending that the crystals being scattered about were to represent the mud, but that finally he came to the conclusion that that was too far fetched and I must say I think it was.

But the great thing is that it is something I said which helped Mr. Hoopington. I was ever so thrilled when I heard that!

You see, Mr. Barraclough said that only one door opened in any of the three rooms, and that was Mr. Spencer going to Mr. Latimer and coming back again. Well, that must have been four doors anyway, but I thought I had heard Mr. Barraclough's door open and someone go in to Mr. Latimer's room and then come back, and I said so. I even said so at the Coroner's inquest, but nobody seemed to take much notice there because they said Mr. Barraclough was in a better position to hear. Well, so he was, but all the time Mr. Hoopington had noticed the point, and in the end it proved that I was right.

I couldn't understand, not quickly, why Mr. Barraclough had added so much to Mr. Latimer's diary, but Mr. Hoopington explained it. I wish he could do the explaining now. He *is* so clever! What he says, is that Mr. Barraclough started with the idea of killing Mr. Spencer and putting the blame on Mr. Latimer, and so getting them both out of the way. Well, I don't think that was at all a nice thing to do, but that's what Mr. Hoopington says he intended to do. Then he got hold of Mr. Latimer's diary and he saw how angry he was and he began to think of the bits he would put in to make it look as if Mr. Latimer had done it. All those bits about the tin and the poison which are ever so complicated and not written a bit like the way Mr. Latimer wrote. Well, all those Mr. Barraclough added. Mr. Hoopington says he added them so as to have his story pat.

You see, the most important thing he thought was to get rid of Mr. Spencer. I don't know why he thought that so strongly, but my woman's instinct told me he hated him, and a woman's instinct is never wrong. I think it was jealousy for a man who was better than what he was.

Then he read what Mr. Spencer wrote and saw the chance of murdering them both and saying they killed each other, and so he did it, and afterwards added the last bit that he pretended Mr. Latimer wrote so as to see he had got all the details right. That Mr. Latimer had sent me out for the *Daily Mail* schedules was a piece of luck he worked in later.

After that he thought he would keep the story up. It meant that he threw himself so fully into the idea of their killing each other, that he almost grew to believe it himself. Also he wanted to put down what Mr. Hoopington said to him to make sure he hadn't made any mistakes, and even there he kept up the pretence with himself, perhaps in case anyone ever found it, because there isn't any proof against him in it; at least I don't think so, but Mr.

Hoopington says there are some bits which might have made him guess.

Then it gets too complicated for me to understand, because not only did he leave a clue, the envelope, to call Mr. Hoopington's attention, as he hoped, to Mr. Latimer, but he put the second tin into Mr. Spencer's drawer. The idea, Mr. Hoopington thinks, was that first of all Mr. Hoopington should be made to think of an accident or suicide, and then of course find out that it wasn't, and then Mr. Barraclough hoped that the police would think that it was Mr. Latimer's idea to deceive them by pretending it was. In other words they were to think that it was Mr. Latimer's way of getting out of the murder if Mr. Spencer alone had been killed. I must say I find it too complicated to follow, but Mr. Hoopington thinks it was rather clever, only rather too clever.

But anyhow, he made a mistake in not leaving Mr. Spencer's writing where it was. Because I told the Inspector about that (me again!) and he couldn't think where it went, but he didn't think it had been thrown out of the window because he thought that he would have found it when he was looking for any more envelopes.

So there it all was. Mr. Hoopington had had his suspicions all the time, but he found them difficult to prove. He says that one of the things that made him convinced that it wasn't Mr. Latimer was that everybody said that Mr. Latimer was so lazy and stupid and feeble. He didn't think he would have had the brains, still less the courage—as a matter of fact he said 'the guts'—to carry all that out. And then again the hitting as he was dying didn't seem the sort of thing that Mr. Spencer would have done. Which of course is quite true.

So he thought that the best thing was to give Mr. Barraclough plenty of rope—well, perhaps under the circumstances that isn't quite a nice phrase to use, but you know what I mean. Well, anyhow, that is why he talked to him for so long and why he let him give such a lot of evidence at the Coroner's inquest, and of course Mr. Hoopington was right. Because in the end Mr. Barraclough over-acted. He kept on pressing his pet theory too hard and forcing the facts to fit it, and there were several little slips, and they all helped.

But it was only that very morning that Mr. Hoopington had got enough evidence to get a warrant and charge him or whatever you do.

Somehow—I don't know how—he had succeeded in tracing the envelope on the balcony and connecting it with him. Well, of course, that was final. It just shows, doesn't it? That it isn't easy to plan a murder and put it on to other people, and I must say I am glad to think that that's true.

Naturally Mr. Hoopington didn't tell us all this then, but he said some of it, just enough for us to know what was going to happen, and then we heard Mr. Barraclough come back into the next room and sit down heavily, as if all the heart had gone out of him.

"All to no purpose! All to no purpose!" we heard him say.

With that, Inspector Hoopington walked straight in and said:

"What was to no purpose?" and I couldn't help it, I followed in afterwards, though Percy did try to stop me.

"Ah, so that woman is to be in at the kill too! You---" and then he called me names that I could not demean myself by repeating. Well, I couldn't write them down anyhow.

But meanwhile Mr. Hoopington arrested him and cautioned him as to what he said. Mr. Barraclough seemed to take no notice.

"Well, anyhow," he said, "let me have the pleasure of sacking these incompetent married nincompoops."

Well, I don't know whatever came over Percy, but he suddenly said:

"I shouldn't do that. Somebody's got to run this business while you're away."

"And you think you'd like to take it over from me, because you know as well as I do I am not coming back; so you hope you can get it for nothing! Well, you're welcome!"

For a moment I thought how lovely it would be. Percy would have been so good and I could have helped him no end! But then I heard Mr. Barraclough's voice go on with a harsh laugh.

"You're welcome, because there isn't any business. Directly I telephoned Tonescu this morning, he knew the game was up. He's just put in his pocket all the money from the sales—I should think it was a good deal—and gone off with it, heaven alone knows where—and we're left to pay all the advertising contracts which *we* have placed. So you're welcome to the business—if you pay its liabilities!"

Well, after that there was a silence.

Then Mr. Barraclough gave a nasty laugh. "Even the cheque I gave to that woman Higgins won't be met—and that's a good thing!"

Then he said: "Ah, I see Miss Wyndham—or should I say Mrs. Thomas? —has stolen my manuscript. Well, she always was an eavesdropping little———"

I don't know what he was going to say, but at that moment Percy hit him hard in the mouth, and quite right too.

He reeled back and then turned to Mr. Hoopington.

"Well, if my staff, my late staff, are going to insult me, it is time to hand myself over to your care. Now that NeO-aD has gone smash, I don't mind. There's nothing left in life worth living for. Get on with it. I'll tell it you all, but for heaven's sake keep that goggle-eyed, rabbit-toothed woman away from me."

Well, that was the last I ever saw of him, and I really don't see why he wanted to be rude. Except of course that I saw him at the trial, and then I could scarcely bring myself to look at him. There wasn't hardly any evidence to give, and he pleaded guilty and wouldn't cross-question anyone. I must say I was rather disappointed. I thought I was going to be the centre of quite a lot of sensation and people would see how well I had done to find him out, and I was quite terrified at the idea of being cross-examined by one of those clever lawyers, though I am sure that my truth and honesty would always have prevailed.

However, there it was. He didn't appeal and there was very little fuss about it at all, and nobody has heard of me or poor Percy, and it has been so difficult to find work, especially for me.

CHAPTER FOUR

Perhaps I ought just to explain as a footnote how I came to have the papers he wrote, and why I have ended it.

You see, as he pleaded guilty, they were never read out, and so they weren't part of the evidence, but when they were likely to be wanted, I got Mr. Hoopington to let me do some work for him by typing out what Mr. Spencer wrote, and as for the rest, in the end I got him to let me keep it. I believe it isn't quite the right thing to do, but still, it is all over and forgotten now, and of course I've changed the names and no one would ever know.

But as for finishing it, that really was Mr. Hoopington's idea too. You see, we being so hard up, I wanted something to do, so he said: "Well, why not take the story and finish it. It will give you something to do, and some day you may be able to publish it, and you might make some money that way. Though not much, I know what these publishers are!"

Well, it was ever so kind of him. But then he always has been kind to us ever since. We call him Uncle George now, and my eldest little boy's been named after him—Percy Hoopington his Christian names are. So that's how I came to take up a literary career, and while murder may not be easy, I must say I think writing is. You just go straight on.

I'm beginning to simply adore it.

THE CASE OF THE FAMISHED PARSON

GEORGE BELLAIRS

THE TOWER ROOM

WEDNESDAY, September 4th. The Cape Mervin Hotel was as quiet as the grave. Everybody was "in" and the night-porter was reading in his cubby-hole under the stairs.

A little hunchbacked fellow was Fennick, with long arms, spindleshanks accentuated by tight, narrow-fitting trousers—somebody's cast-offs—and big feet. Some disease had robbed him of all his hair. He didn't need to shave and when he showed himself in public, he wore a wig. The latter was now lying on a chair, as though Fennick had scalped himself for relief.

The plainwood table was littered with papers and periodicals left behind by guests and rescued by the porter from the salvage dump. He spent a lot of his time reading and never remembered what he had read.

Two or three dailies, some illustrated weeklies of the cheaper variety, and a copy of Old Moore's Almanac. A sporting paper and a partly completed football pool form. . . .

Fennick was reading "What the Stars have in Store." He was breathing hard and one side of his face was contorted with concentration. He gathered that the omens were favourable.

Venus and Jupiter in good aspect. Success in love affairs and a promising career.... He felt better for it.

Outside the tide was out. The boats in the river were aground. The light in the tower at the end of the break-water changed from white to red and back at minute intervals. The wind blew up the gravel drive leading from the quayside to the hotel and tossed bits of paper and dead leaves about. Down below on the road to the breakwater you could see the coke glowing in a brazier and the silhouette of a watchman's cabin nearby.

The clock on the Jubilee Tower on the promenade across the river struck midnight. At this signal the grandfather clocks in the public rooms and hall began to chime all at once in appalling discord, like a peal of bells being 'fired.' The owner of the hotel was keen on antiques and bric-a-brac and meticulously oiled and regulated all his clocks himself.

Then, in mockery of the ponderous timepieces, a clock some-where else cuckooed a dozen times. The under-manager, who had a sense of humour, kept it in his office, set to operate just after the heavy ones. Most people laughed at it. So far, the proprietor hadn't seen the point.

Fennick stirred himself, blinked his hairless eyelids, laid aside the oracle, stroked his naked head as though soothing it after absorbing so much of the future, and rose to lock the main door. Then he entered the bar.

The barmaid and cocktail-shaker had been gone almost an hour. Used glasses stood around waiting to be washed first thing in the morning. The night-porter took a tankard from a hook and emptied all the dregs from the glasses into it. Beer, stout, gin, whisky, vermouth.... A good pint of it.... One hand behind his back, he drank without stopping, his prominent Adam's-apple and dewlaps agitating, until it was all gone. Then he wiped his mouth on the back of his hand, sighed with satisfaction, selected and lighted the largest cigarette-end from one of the many ash-trays scattered about and went off to his next job.

It was the rule that Fennick collected all shoes, chalked their room-numbers on their soles and carried them to the basement for cleaning. But he had ways of his own. He took a large newspaper and his box of cleaning materials and silently dealt with the footwear, one by one, as it stood outside the doors of the bedrooms, spreading the paper to protect the carpet.

Fennick started for the first floor. Rooms 1, 2, 3, 4 and 5, with the best views over the river and bay. His gait was jaunty, for he had had a few beers before finally fuddling himself with the dregs from the bar. He hummed a tune to himself.

> Don't send my boy to prizzen,
> It's the first crime wot he's done....

He tottered up the main staircase with his cleaning-box and stopped at the first door.

Number 1 was a single room. Once it had been double, but the need for more bathrooms had split it in two. Outside, on the mat, a pair of substantial handmade black shoes. Fennick glided his two brushes and polishing-cloth over them with hasty approval. They belonged to Judge Tennant, of the High Court. He came every year at this time for a fishing holiday. He tipped meticulously. Neither too much not too little. Yet you didn't mind. You felt justice had been done when you got it.

Fennick had been sitting on his haunches. Now and then he cocked an ear to make sure that nobody was stirring. He moved like a crab to Number 2 gently dragging his tackle along with him.

This was the best room, with a private bath. Let to a millionaire, they said. It was a double, and in the register the occupants had gone down as Mr. and Mrs. Cuhady. All the staff, from the head waiter down to the handyman who raked the gravel round the hotel and washed down the cars, knew it was a lie. The head waiter was an expert on that sort of thing. With thirty years' experience in a dining-room you can soon size-up a situation.

That was how they knew about the honeymoon couple in Number 3, too. Outside their door was a pair of new men's brogues and some new brown suede ladies' shoes. "The Bride's travelling costume consisted of … with brown suede shoes…." Fennick knew all about it from reading his papers in the small hours.

There were five pairs of women's shoes outside Number 2. Brown leather, blue suede, black and red tops, light patent leather, and a pair with silk uppers. All expensive ones.

Five pairs in a day! Fennick snarled and showed a nasty gap where he had lost four teeth. Just like her! He cleaned the brown, the black-and-red and the patent uppers with the same brushes for spite. The blue suede he ignored altogether. And he spat contemptuously on the silk ones and wiped them with a dirty cloth.

Mr. Cuhady seemed to have forgotten his shoes altogether. That was a great relief! He was very particular about them. Lovely hand-made ones and the colour of old mahogany. And you had to do them properly, or he played merry hell. Mr. Cuhady had blood-pressure and "Mrs." Cuhady didn't seem to be doing it any good. The magnate was snoring his head off. There was no other sound in Number 2. Fennick bet himself that his partner was noiselessly rifling Cuhady's pocket-book….

He crawled along and dealt with the honeymoon shoes. They weren't too good. Probably they'd saved-up hard to have their first nights together at a posh hotel and would remember it all their lives. "Remember the Cape Mervin … ?" Fennick, sentimental under his mixed load of drinks, spat on all four soles for good luck…. He crept on.

Two pairs of brogues this time. Male and female. Good ones, too, and well cared for. Fennick handled them both with reverence. A right good job. For he had read a lot in his papers about one of the occupants of Room 4. An illustrated weekly had even interviewed him at Scotland Yard and printed his picture.

On the other side of the door were two beds, separated by a table on which stood a reading-lamp, a travelling-clock and two empty milk glasses. In one bed a good-looking, middle-aged woman was sitting-up, with a dressing-gown round her shoulders, reading a book about George Sand.

In the other a man was sleeping on his back. On his nose a pair of horn-rimmed spectacles; on the eiderdown a thriller had fallen from his limp hand. He wore striped silk pyjamas and his mouth was slightly open.

The woman rose, removed the man's glasses and book, drew the bedclothes over his arms, kissed him lightly on his thinning hair, and then climbed back into bed and resumed her reading. Inspector Littlejohn slept on....

Fennick had reached the last room of the block. Number 5 was the tower room. The front of the Cape Mervin Hotel was like a castle. A wing, a tower, the main block, a second tower, and then another wing. Number 5 was in the left-hand tower. And it was occupied at the time by the Bishop of Greyle and his wife.

As a rule there were two pairs here, too. Heavy, brown serviceable shoes for Mrs. Bishop; boots, dusty, with solid, heavy soles and curled-up toes, for His Lordship. Tonight there was only one pair. Mrs. Greyle's. Nobody properly knew the bishop's surname. He signed everything "J. C. Greyle" and they didn't like to ask his real name. Somebody thought it was Macintosh.

Fennick was so immersed in his speculations that he didn't see the door open. Suddenly looking up he found Mrs. Greyle standing there in a blue dressing-gown staring down at him.

The night-porter hastily placed his hand flat on the top of his head to cover his nakedness, for he'd forgotten his wig. He felt to have a substantial thatch of hair now, however, and every hair of his head seemed to rise.

"Have you seen my husband?" said Mrs. Greyle, or Macintosh, or whatever it was. "He went out at eleven and hasn't returned."

Fennick writhed from his haunches to his knees and then to his feet, like a prizefighter who has been down.

"No, mum … I don't usually do the boots this way, but I'm so late, see?"

"Wherever can he be …? So unusual…."

She had a net over her grey hair. Her face was white and drawn. It must have been a very pretty face years ago…. Her hands trembled as she clutched her gown to her.

"Anything I can do, mum?"

"I can't see that there is. I don't know where he's gone. The telephone in our room rang at a quarter to eleven and he just said he had to go out and wouldn't be long. He didn't explain…."

"Oh, he'll be turnin' up. P'raps visitin' the sick, mum."

Fennick was eager to be off. The manager's quarters were just above and if he got roused and found out Fennick's little cleaning dodge, it would be, as the porter inwardly told himself, Napooh!

It was no different the following morning, when the hotel woke up. The bishop was still missing.

At nine o'clock things began to happen.

First, the millionaire sent for the manager and raised the roof.

His shoes were dirty. Last night he'd put them out as usual to be cleaned. This morning he had found them, not only uncleaned, but twice as dirty as he'd left them. In fact, muddy right up to the laces. He demanded an immediate personal interview with the proprietor. Somebody was going to get fired for it….

"Mrs." Cuhady, who liked to see other people being bullied and pushed around, watched with growing pride and satisfaction the magnate's mounting blood-pressure…

At nine-fifteen they took the bishop's corpse to the town morgue in the ambulance. He had been found at the bottom of Bolter's Hole, with the tide lapping round his emaciated body and his head bashed in.

The first that most of the guests knew of something unusual was the appearance of the proprietor in the dining-room just after nine. This was extraordinary, for Mr. Allain was a lazy man with a reputation for staying in bed until after ten.

Mr. Allain, a tall fat man and usually imperturbable, appeared unshaven and looking distracted. After a few words with the head waiter, who pointed out a man eating an omelette at a table near the window, he waddled across the room.

They only got bacon once a week at the Cape Mervin and Littlejohn was tackling an omelette without enthusiasm. His wife was reading a letter from her sister at Melton Mowbray who had just had another child.

Mr. Allain whispered to Littlejohn. All eyes in the room turned in their direction. Littlejohn emptied his mouth and could be seen mildly arguing. In response, Mr. Allain, who was half French, clasped his hands in entreaty. So, Littlejohn, after a word to his wife, left the room with the proprietor….

"Something must have happened," said the guests one to another.

WANT ANOTHER PERFECT MYSTERY?

Get your next classic crime story for free...

Sign up to our Crime Classics newsletter where you can discover new Golden Age crime, receive exclusive content and never-before published short stories, all for free.

From the beloved greats of the Golden Age to the forgotten gems, best-kept-secrets, and brand new discoveries, we're devoted to classic crime.

If you sign up today, you'll get:

1. A free novel from our Classic Crime collection.
2. Exclusive insights into classic novels and their authors and the chance to get copies in advance of publication, and
3. The chance to win exclusive prizes in regular competitions.

Interested? It takes less than a minute to sign up. You can get your novel and your first newsletter by signing up on our website www.crimeclassics.co.uk